The
Witness

... living a lie!

MARY JANE FORBES

Todd Book Publications

The WITNESS

ISBN: 978-0615951591 (sc)
Printed in the United States of America
Todd Book Publications: 11/2013
Second release: 1/2014
Port Orange, Florida

Author photo: Ami Ringeisen Floyd
Cover design 2018 by Angie: pro_ebookcovers

To Peggy,

Always up for a scouting excursion! This time it was the southern towns of Maine, including a stop for coffee at the Bagel Basket, and the rediscovery of the bakery, When Pigs Fly.

So much fun!

MAPS

Maine

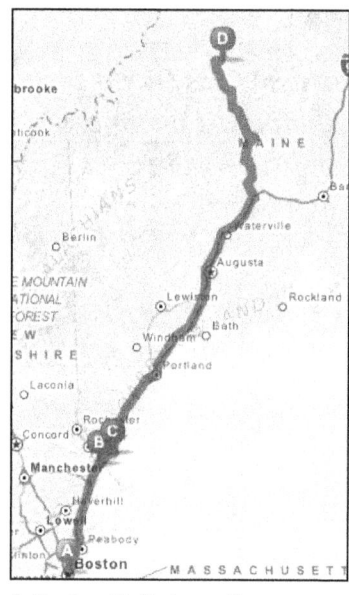

A: Boston, **B:** Portsmouth,
C: York, **D:** Moosehead Lake

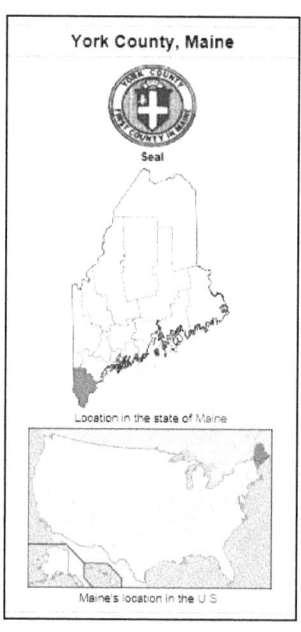

Mexico

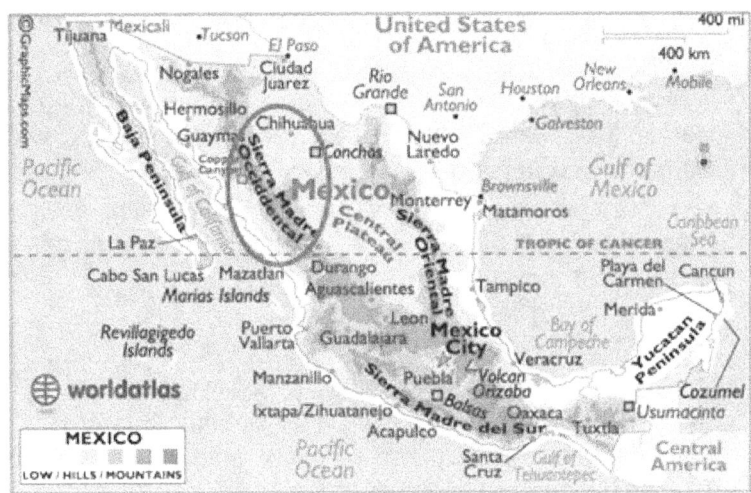

Florida

Cast

Witness
Dr. Maria Grayson
Morgan Grant (alias)
Marianne Grayson: Maria's Mom

Feds
Agent Alex Donovan
U.S. Marshal Zachary Vickers

The Macintyres
Charles Daniel Macintyre (Mac)
Daniel Macintyre: Mac's Pops
Patty Sue: Name of Mac's boat
Mac's Crew: Sissy, Studs

Florida Friends
Elizabeth Stitchway, PI
Manny Salinas, PI
Madame Crystal: Psychic

York Maine
Dr. Joe Bartholomew
Dr. Richard Farnsworth
Harriet
Stella Trent
Howard Bond

Mexico
Junior DelaCruz:
leader DelaCruz cartel

Felix Mendoza: Junior's
lieutenant

Wally Gutfeld: dead,
was Junior's lieutenant

The
Witness

... living a lie!

Chapter 1

THERE HE WAS ON the beach, looking up at the house. The albino. Waves from the tropical storm roared behind him, his white skin, white hair, and pink eyes seeking her blood, her death. He was after her, to silence her once and for all.

Only she could identify him. He had to eliminate her. He had to kill her. She had seen the murder. Witnessed him kill his rival competitor.

Standing at the French door, she bent her head to the cool glass, nerves pinging through her body, body trembling.

"What am I going to do?" she whispered, her auburn hair falling over her eyes.

The howling winds of the tropical storm buffeted the door, bent trees to the breaking point, black clouds turning early evening to night. Heavy rain turned roads to streams. The stench of seaweed mixed with the salty sea and the decomposing vegetation under the trees.

What am I going to do? For two years I felt safe, watched the news, read the headlines … he didn't know where I was. Then Donovan arrived. The Federal Agent had pieces of a puzzle, said that together, with me as a star, no, a critical witness, he could start the process to bring down the Mexican cartel running guns, smuggling drugs—not because they confiscated the contraband crossing the border, oh no, because I saw the leader commit murder. I know what to do … but do I have to? Do I have the courage?

The questions pulsating in her brain, Maria ran to the bedroom, pulled a travel case from under the bed. Running her fingers over the lock she paused, then pushed the button releasing the lid. Bundles of ten and twenty dollar bills were stacked neatly inside. Her heart beating wildly against her chest, she slammed the top down. Dropping to her knees, Maria yanked out a larger case. *This is all so silly. I'm not going to do this. I'm not going to run away.*

She unzipped a side pocket of the case, lifted the velvet pouch letting a gold chain holding a gold cross with a single ruby in the center fall into the palm of her hand. Along with the chain and cross, a small conch shell rolled onto her fingers. Her face flushed with the memory of Mac making love to her on a sandbar, a sandbar where he had picked up the small shell placing it in her hand.

Fear suddenly ripped through her hands, through her body. Holding the shell and the memory, how could she risk putting Mac in danger? Danger of being caught unexpectedly in a crossfire, bullets intended for her. Attaching the chain around her neck, slipping the cross under her white silk blouse, she returned the shell to the little bag.

Suddenly, a bolt of lightning filled the sky. Maria held her breath. The crack was instant, close by. Along with the lightning came the realization that she was not safe, but could she really do it? Leave her life here, her life as a surgeon, leave Mac?

She forced herself to breathe deeply … breathe … breathe … breathe.

Her body quivering, she returned to the French door, looked out at the railing bordering the narrow deck, out over the silhouette of trees, out to the beach, the roar of the pounding surf penetrating the glass.

She hadn't revealed everything, didn't tell Agent Donovan everything she saw that day two years ago. She'd held back, hoping she wouldn't be pulled into his investigation. Hadn't told him she would never forget the man in the white coat, striped pants. Never forget his face—pure white skin, white hair, and his eyes, pink eyes, blood filling the capillaries of the iris. She had expunged his image from her mind earlier today, as she stood next to Mac, both staring in disbelief at the boat careening toward them.

It was him.

The albino had found her.

She gave Mac a searing kiss leaving him standing on the dock as she raced home.

Another bolt of lightning, bigger than the last, turned night to day. Maria's eyes filled with terror. Lightning, followed by claps of thunder, struck the palm trees lining the path from the beach, illuminating his progress toward the house, his silvery hair glistening in the streak of electricity.

Trembling, Maria traced her lips with her fingers, felt the heat of Mac's lips on hers. Felt the strength of his arms around her. Felt the searing kiss knowing in her heart she was saying goodbye. She had to leave him. He was in danger because of her.

Fumbling for her cell, she tapped the code, lifted the tiny lifeline to her ear. The call was answered before the first ring ended.

"Donovan here."

"I'm ready. I'll do it. The albino … he's here."

"Oh, my God. Where?"

"On the path from the beach."

"Thank God you called. Don't go outside, Dr. Grayson. I'm only a few houses away—we've been watching you. I repeat, do not go outside. Wait! Don't open the door until you hear my voice—code word: chapel. Three minutes. Don't call anyone. Your life is at stake! Three minutes."

Maria didn't close her cell. One call. She had to make one call.

"Hello, Sunrise House."

"This is Dr. Grayson. I have to speak to my mother."

"I'm so sorry, Dr. Grayson. She's been very agitated today for some reason. We gave her a sedative to calm her down. She's asleep."

"Please, I must talk to her. Check. Maybe she's awake."

… a bolt of lightning, crack of thunder, darkness.

"Hello."

"Mother, it's me, Maria."

"Who?"

"Your daughter. Maria. I love you, Mother."

Maria disconnected the call.

At that moment Dr. Maria Grayson left one life to begin another—a witness to murder.

Chapter 2

THE WIND CONTINUED TO howl, whipping the two black SUVs as they sped through the driving rain to Tampa International Airport.

Sitting next to his witness in the back seat of the lead car, Agent Donovan spoke softly into his cell, his eyes fixed on the back of his driver's head, listening, then spitting orders, then listening again. His body stiffened, breathing seemed to stop. Suddenly he slapped the cell between his palms, eyes remaining on his driver. Time passed. He lifted the cell again to his ear, listened, then relayed identification and instructions to the guard station.

As the vehicles approached, the gate opened then shut behind the cars as they raced to the military jet waiting on the tarmac. The plane's nose, tail, and wing lights blinked eerily through the sheets of rain accompanied by the piercing sound of engines ready to take flight.

Donovan, a spot on his shaved bald head reflecting a light from the tip of the wing, escorted Maria to the plane as another agent scrambled from the second car, yanked Maria's suitcases from the trunk, and quickly handed them off to an officer waiting at the foot of the stairs leading up to the plane's open door.

Within minutes the plane was airborne. Rain pelted the windows. But not for long as the silver U.S. Air Force jet climbed through the clouds silhouetting Maria in the moonlight. Agent Donovan patted her hand. "Would you like something to eat? Drink?" It was the first time he had spoken to her since she opened the front door responding to the code word *chapel*. She shook her head, no.

"We'll be setting down briefly at Andrew's Air Force Base outside of Washington. U.S. Marshal Zachary Vickers has been assigned to your case. I will leave you at Andrews, but I'll be in touch from time to time … to see how you're adjusting. I know you have many questions. Marshal Vickers will give you the answers. He will brief you on everything."

The pilot sent word to his passengers to prepare for landing in ten minutes. The plane set down light as a feather and taxied to an open hangar. In the shadow of the structure, a man holding a briefcase stood waiting.

"Maria, you did the right thing. Give your new life a chance. I wish you the best," Donovan said.

"My new life? Sounds so permanent."

The agent smiled looking into her violet eyes, and then he was gone, passing a gentleman in the doorway at the top of the stairs leading down to the tarmac. They exchanged words, shook hands, and then the stranger dressed in a black suit, white shirt open at the neck, ambled up to Maria. Smiling, he sat next to her, buckled his seatbelt, and within minutes the jet was airborne again.

"Hi, I'm Marshal Zachary Vickers. I'm your friend."

Maria shot him a furtive glance, then turned to the window, her hands folded on her lap, then gripping the arms of the seat, then one hand in her lap. Out of the corner of her eyes she stole a glimpse at the man sitting next to her, then back to the window.

Noting her gestures, he put his hand on her elbow resting on the arm between their seats. He turned to her and, with a slight smile, spoke in a soft voice. "We have to talk, Maria. There's a conference room stocked with snacks and some drinks. Please, follow me."

Unbuckling her seatbelt, Maria rose and dutifully followed the marshal into a brightly lit room. There were no windows. Six chairs, three to a side, were pushed up to a highly polished honey-oak table anchored to the floor in the middle of the space. A mini bar was in the corner—a plate of sandwiches covered with plastic wrap, napkins, and two cups sat on the small counter.

Maria stared at the scene. She felt like a movie star in a grim mystery film.

Vickers rolled a black leather chair out for her then walked to the opposite side of the table and sat in another of the chairs. Lying on the table in front of him was a manila folder which he opened revealing a sheaf of papers. Pushing his black horn-rimmed glasses up on his nose, he looked across the table at Maria. He sighed, leaned forward.

"Are you okay?" he asked.

"I think so. I've stopped shaking. I'm not going to bolt out of the emergency exit if that's what you want to hear. Where are we going?" she asked.

"That's what we have to talk about. I have papers for you to sign, others to read. Guidelines for what you are expected to do. And, what you can expect from us. Agent Donovan anticipated you would ask for protection. In return for that protection, we look for your testimony when the time is right."

"When the time is right? I thought you would ask for my testimony … but I also thought it would be relatively soon."

"Not exactly. We have more evidence to gather for the case. It could be months, or, Maria, it could be a few years," he said looking over his glasses.

Maria jumped to her feet but the plane hit some turbulence knocking her back into the chair. "Hey, I didn't sign on for … for years."

"The DelaCruz gang is ruthless. When they realize you have disappeared, hear about your car incinerating, we assume they won't buy our story that you are dead. We believe they will guess you are in protective custody. They will stop at nothing … do you hear me … nothing to prevent you from testifying. The fact you can place the albino … his name is Camacho DelaCruz known as Junior … in the hospital room and saw him turn off the equipment keeping Arturo Perez alive, thereby killing his arch rival, he will know your testimony can put him away for life, maybe death row, for the murder. You did see him didn't you?"

Maria looked down at her hands, a slight tremor again, then up at Vickers. "Yes."

"We have one new piece of evidence … no, not evidence yet. Agent Donovan's forensic team took three sets of prints from the room in Cortez, Florida where they found two murdered men, known as Studs and Wally. Prints from the victims. The third set of prints hasn't been identified, could be Junior's. Our theory, given you saw him out in the Gulf when he almost rammed the boat you and the fisherman were in, is that he killed the two. They had become liabilities. Of course, that's all just a theory. We haven't been able to get Junior's prints. Something we're working on. Now, shall we execute these documents?"

"Yes." Maria sighed.

Vickers hesitated, ran his fingers over his shaved bald scalp as he looked at Maria, compassion in his eyes. "These first few hours will be difficult. I know from talking with other witnesses. You've been plucked from a life you worked hard for—friends, family, people close to you—for a life ahead that is unknown. I'm going to help you with your new life as much as I can. But you have to do the hard work ... hit the unknown head on."

So, Maria thought, at the age of thirty-six I start a new life, leave behind who I was for a new person, a person I'll become. Donovan and now Vickers said they'd help me. My life is in the hands of two bald-headed agents? She sat straight in the chair exhibiting the calm composure of a confident woman, willing her hands to be still. But, inside she was in turmoil—anxiety coupled with fear twisting her stomach, her heart, and her mind in knots.

Maria stared at Vickers.

He braced himself for what was coming.

"What happened ... back at the house? Agent Donovan grabbed my keys and then practically threw me into the car, talked on his cell until we arrived at the airport. He seemed upset."

"When you called Donovan, telling him you saw the albino on the path, he immediately dispatched his agents to find him. They swarmed the grounds, the path, up and down the beach—"

"Did they catch him? It's over?" Maybe all of this is for nothing. I can go back—

"No. The storm, so dark—he slipped away like a chameleon, changing the color of his skin from white to black. Donovan was sure the agents would find him ... but ... he vanished. I'm sorry."

Maria looked down at the table.

"There's one more thing. As you left the house, an agent, a woman, immediately took your car, drove up I-75. She was followed closely by another agent. At a turn in the road she stopped. She and the other agent then staged an accident. Your car was incinerated. When it's found, identified, the report will be that you died in the car."

Maria gasped. Mac … Mac would not think she had disappeared … he would believe she was dead. Maria continued to stare at Vickers.

Vickers didn't move.

His words hit Maria in her gut.

The drone of the jet's engines filled the room.

Marshal Zachary Vickers looked away, took a deep breath, and then picked up the top document placing it in front of Maria along with a pen. "From this moment on Dr. Maria Grayson ceases to exist. You are now Morgan Grant—same initials to help in the transition. Your identity as a doctor will not be known by those you come into contact with until you *and* I feel it is appropriate. You are being relocated to York, Maine … far away from the southern states and Mexico, where we believe Junior DelaCruz calls home."

Maria, still reeling from what he told her, fought for composure, fought to fill her lungs with air as she began to realize the magnitude of what was happening to her.

Vickers handed Morgan several more pages. "Please read these, memorize them. Morgan Grant's background. You are a nurse practitioner from Wenatchee, a city on the eastern side of a mountain range in Washington State. Your parents are dead. No siblings. You wanted to get away from the heartache of losing your parents who died in a terrible automobile accident. You have always wanted to experience life in New England.

"We've rented a small house for you in the center of town. A job interview is scheduled. You don't have to accept the offer that will come your way, but I suggest you take the opportunity initially to give you some time to get your sea legs so to speak. The job, in a private practice, will be offered by Dr. Richard Farnsworth—a family doctor. A nice older physician, whose nurse practitioner suddenly quit to be married in California. Your job will be to assist Farnsworth until he finds a replacement which, if it works out, could be you."

"May I remind you, I *am* a doctor, a *surgeon*."

"I know, but in the meantime, you will interview in a few days with Farnsworth as a nurse practitioner. If you like each other, which I'm sure you will, you will start work the following week."

"Do you have something besides soda? I think I'd like a drink and one of those sandwiches. I haven't eaten since … I can't remember when," Morgan said with a sigh, tamping down the anger boiling up inside her, trying not to rebel against what the marshal was saying.

"Certainly. How does what I've said so far sound?"

Morgan watched him pick up a bottle of wine.

With no response, the marshal turned. Maybe she didn't hear him. He looked into her blank stare. "In the past, we've found that if a witness can adapt, can embrace their new situation … your participation in witness protection … you may grow to like your new life." Vickers poured two glasses of white wine, raised his glass to hers. "Here's to your new adventure."

Morgan sipped the wine, took a bite of the ham sandwich, and then pushed it aside. She had lost her appetite.

Chapter 3

York, Maine
August twenty-first

A SOFT BREEZE FLUTTERED the white curtain in rhythm to the beat of the crickets' wings. Morgan pulled the lacey fabric to the side releasing a moonbeam across the highly polished oak floorboards. Curling up on the cushioned window seat, she marveled at the stillness, feeling the velvety night cloak her in its soft embrace.

Marshal Vickers brought her to this house, to her new home.

It was after three when she said goodnight to the marshal, pulled herself up the stairs and laid down on the bed. She had no strength to remove the tan capris or white blouse, the clothes she wore when she fled Anna Maria Island, fled in the storm battering the coastline, fled from the man intent on killing her.

The sound of the crickets had drawn her to the window. The beauty of the night, the stars twinkling … promising what? A new beginning? That's what Vickers said. She didn't want a new beginning. She had always wanted to be a doctor, been driven toward that goal and worked hard to achieve it. She had a good life but that all changed with the unintended consequence of passing a patient's open door, the consequence of becoming a witness to a murder.

Morgan Grant? So, that was her new name. "Should I fight to be released from this new circumstance? To what end? To be killed?" she whispered to the owl, his soft hoo-hoo floating to her on the breeze. "Better to what … what was it Vickers said? 'Embrace your new life. Think of it as an adventure.'"

I've never had time to think of adventure—only two years out of my residency, off to a new position at the Manatee Memorial Hospital and the challenging ER unit in Bradenton. On the other hand, it might be nice to relax in a family practice. Meet patients, have time to talk to them, look into their eyes—find a way to relieve the pain that lay behind their blank stare.

Dawn would break soon. All she had seen were silhouettes of tall trees, the entrance to this little house, and Vickers' back as she followed him up the stairs dragging her suitcases. He said she should get some sleep. He'd fix coffee in the morning, her first day as Morgan Grant. They'd talk more then.

There was maybe two hours before she would learn more of her fate. Until then she had to get her thoughts together. Tomorrow was going to be a struggle between the old and the new. Mac. What about Mac? She felt they were falling in love ... slow and easy. They had made love once. No, that was not love. It was pent up passion. But wasn't love around the corner?

Over. That was over. But she could see his face, feel his arms, feels his lips when she turned and fiercely kissed him goodbye standing on the dock. After seeing the albino heading full throttle at them, heading to ram and sink their boat, to kill her, she made the decision that moment to seek the protective custody that had been offered. She just didn't know if her decision would stick.

Padding into the bathroom, she turned on the light, looked into the mirror over the vanity. If she was going to be born again at age thirty-six, come into this life as a grown woman, then she had to see someone else in the mirror. Smiling, she pulled a lock of her long auburn hair forward. *Blonde. Yes, they say blondes have more fun.* Well, she'd find out. And her eyes—violet. *They will have to change. Brown, soft brown would be nice.*

If she didn't recognize the new woman in the mirror then she'd feel safe. The killer wouldn't recognize her either.

A sudden exhaustion seeped through every pore of her body. Struggling to keep her eyes open she sought the bed in the moonlight and stretched out on the soft quilt. Her lids shut blocking out the terror of the previous twenty-four hours. Relaxed, Morgan Grant fell into a deep, dreamless sleep.

Chapter 4

MORGAN GRANT WAS BORN on a beautiful summer morning.

Slowly her senses came to life as the aroma of coffee tickled her nose.

Morgan opened her eyes letting them rove over the room. A bank of windows lined up against one wall. The bench she sat on a few hours earlier was under one of them, and then a maple dresser with a small porcelain lamp topped with a hurricane shade. The room was papered with tiny light-blue flowers; the quilt covering her had bouquets of yellow and blue flowers, hand stitched with love. A rocking chair with a braided seat pad was between another bank of three windows and a second dresser.

Drained, yet somewhat refreshed with the few hours of sleep, she returned to the window seat. Now, in the bright morning sun, she gazed down on a flowerbed bordering the house, then a small expanse of lawn fringed with tall trees—maple, oak, chestnut, and pine with underbrush curling around the base of the trunks. Birds sang to each other, calling to her to come out and play. If Maria Grayson died in Florida, then Morgan Grant was born into a new heaven filled with birds and flowers.

Her nerves spiked. She was over fifteen-hundred miles from her old life. Breathing deep several times, she succeeded in tamping down some of her apprehension.

Responding to the rich aroma of coffee, she glanced in the mirror to see who looked back at her. Yes, she had work to do. Turning away from the person in the mirror she stepped with bare feet down the soft yet worn braided stair treads. At the foot of the stairs she stopped. She had seen movies filmed in New England, and what she saw before her was most certainly a classic movie set.

"Hey, good morning." Zachary Vickers was dressed in the same black suit from the night before, but he had kicked off his shoes, a simple act. They were settling into a comfortable family relationship. At least that's how Morgan saw it. In spite of his boyish grin and sock feet, he was ready for business. "I ran to the Bagel Basket and picked up some breakfast along with several cups of strong coffee, which I'm sure you could use after last night. I didn't know how you liked it but there are creamers and sugar packets on the counter. Why don't you look around while I set up shop on the little deck off the kitchen. There's a table and a few chairs. We can eat and talk there." He said all this while she stared at him accepting the mug of coffee he held out to her.

Smiling, he returned to the kitchen, calling over his shoulder. "If it's okay with you I'll hang around until this afternoon … help you settle in. Then I have to head back to Boston, the field office, but not until I've answered all your questions. Plus we have some basic things to address."

Morgan followed him through the kitchen taking note of the pine cabinets, pale yellow walls, red brick linoleum floor leading out to the deck that he had mentioned. "This house is very cozy. Who owns it?"

"A widow lady, eighty-one. She and her husband bought the house in 1970. He died last year and her son moved her into a retirement home. I understand she's sharp as a tack but has a heart condition. He was concerned about her living out here alone but she wouldn't agree to sell … not yet anyway. The house held too many memories."

Morgan sipped her coffee as she stepped from the deck onto the lush lawn, turned to look at the house. It was just as charming on the outside—yellow clapboard with flowerbeds around the foundation, a split-rail fence separating the front lawn from the narrow road. Looking right and left, she returned to the round weathered-pine table. "So many flowerbeds. How did they manage?"

"Mr. Thaxter was a botanist. The professor taught at the University of New Hampshire in Durham, near Portsmouth—"

"Sounds like quite a commute."

"Not really. Maybe thirty minutes … more if it's tourist season—summer and winter … skiing in the winter."

"The Thaxter's son, where is he?"

"A border guard based in Texas. He'll be retiring in a couple of years. I met him when we signed the rental agreement."

"How far is Boston, your field office?"

"An hour and a half, more if it's tourist season," he chuckled. "But I-95 is a direct shot."

"Marshal Vickers—"

"How about calling me Zach?"

"Okay, Zach, I have two things to do this morning—the beauty shop and an optometrist, and don't ask me why," Morgan said with a grin.

"All right, I won't. I get the hair thing, although you look great, especially considering—"

Morgan cut him off. She had no desire to revisit the *considering*. She felt relaxed and didn't want to kick up the nerves. "I need a map and a phonebook."

"... and a way to get around." There was a cardboard box on the chair next to him. Opening it he pulled out a file folder. "Here's a detailed map of York Village, half a mile east from here. A telephone directory is on the kitchen table. Here's a set of keys—front door, back door, garage, and car. There's a 1995 Oldsmobile equipped with a GPS in the garage. According to junior it runs pretty good ... it's a start. Morgan, what's the matter."

Morgan's face tightened as she stared back him. She didn't answer but he realized what he had said. The word *junior*. Zachary sighed. He knew from talking to others he had relocated, that crazy things crop up from their past scuttling their nerves. Junior was what the albino was known by. He decided not to respond to her fear. She was going to have to face these random coincidences.

"You didn't have groceries on your list," he said. "How about I pick up enough to see you through for a couple of days ... then ... you're on your own. Are you going to be okay?"

"Yes, I'll be okay." This time she didn't smile but the tension in her shoulders relaxed. This was not heaven. *Mac.* She longed to hear his voice. *What was he thinking? Did he believe she was dead?*

"Before you head out to have your hair done, read over the first page, a summary of your background—details are on the following pages. The synopsis will cover questions you're apt to be asked: moved here from Wenatchee, sudden death of your parents, wanted to get far away—too painful, nurse practitioner; and yes you have a Maine nurse's license. Naturally, you will adlib, expanding your descriptions. A tip that other witnesses have suggested is to think of something that actually happened to you in your prior life, something that fits the narrative in your new identity. They say this trick makes it easier to remember what you said. By the way, if you want to practice as a doctor, you will have to take the State Boards. Okay?"

"Yes, and the sooner the better."

Zach handed her another file. "All the information pertaining to practicing in Maine is in here—forms, contacts, dates."

"You marshals seem to have thought of everything," she said leafing through the pages.

"Not everything. Things will happen you'll have to deal with, especially the first few days and weeks. It's not going to be easy, Morgan. As I said last night—try not to give in to your instincts to fight what has happened to you. Try to embrace the opportunity. Here's your new cell phone. My number is stored under my name, Zach. Call me anytime—day or night. I'll help you. I'm less than two hours away. Now, let's tackle a few practical matters. More coffee?"

"I'll get it," Morgan said. "You organize the practical file folders."

Returning, she set their mugs on the table, then leaned against the wood railing circling the deck gazing out at the lush forest. Wrapping her arms around her body, closing her eyes, she inhaled the sweet air of morning. *Not so bad,* she thought. *Feels safe.* "Okay, I'm ready."

"I hope you don't mind, but Agent Donovan checked your bags. Just a precaution. The hundred grand … did you close the bank accounts?"

"No. I'm not even sure why I withdrew the money. I suppose in the back of my mind I knew I was leaving the area … one way or the other."

"I'll see that they're closed today. If there's a balance we'll return it to you. Any other accounts? Investments?"

"No, that's it."

"Today or tomorrow, soon, open an account at a local bank. Use your relocation story—parents died, painful, wanted a fresh start. Here's your new social security card—keep it with you until you're sure you remember it correctly. Your social, new name and address—easy to make a slip. It's up to you to handle all the things you would have installed when making a move—telephone, television and internet. Remember, don't contact anyone connected with your past. The document you signed on the plane—we will protect you but only if you stay in your new identity. If we find you have violated that rule, you will be on your own."

"My mother—"

"I'll give you weekly updates for a month then only at your request. The clothes you packed will be good for another couple of months, then, lucky you, it will be time for a new *winter* wardrobe. You'll love the fall here. Ever been to New England in the fall—the colors?"

"No to the colors, no to New England, but from the looks of it, I think I'll like it," Morgan said glancing at the flowers ablaze in orange, blue, and gold against the edge of the deck.

"I just hope you like it when the flowers are gone and there's three feet of snow on the ground. By the way, Paul Thaxter, the son, said a gardener mows the lawn once a week and periodically tends the flowerbeds until the snow falls. A snow removal service will keep the driveway clear. I guess the service has been on contract to the Thaxter's for several years."

Zach paused, shoved his glasses up on his nose. "Donovan also saw your gun. Were you trained to handle it?"

"Yes. And, I was told by the instructor where I bought it— training was mandatory—that I was above average. I passed."

Morgan drank the last drop of her coffee and looked at Zach, his horn-rimmed glasses perched squarely on his nose. "Well, Marshal Zachary Vickers, I think it's time for me to shower, change into some fresh clothes, and then venture out into my new life. Can you add dishwasher soap to your grocery list?"

"Will do, and please, as I suggested, call me Zach. The marshal moniker can get in the way. If by any chance you have to explain who I am, just say I'm an old college friend. Have fun and remember four words."

Morgan looked at him quizzically.

"If you want to redirect the conversation away from you ... *and, how about you?* One last warning. If you see someone you know, turn the other way … put distance between you and the other person immediately!"

Chapter 5

WITH TWO THOUSAND DOLLARS of crisp bills in her purse, along with some change, her new social security card, and the phonebook, Morgan sucked in a big gulp of air and headed out for the beauty shop that was circled in the phonebook's yellow pages. Adjusting the rearview mirror, she backed out of the garage, down the driveway and out onto Scituate Road. Catching her reflection in the mirror, she pulled a flyaway lock of hair, auburn hair, behind her ear. "Blondie, here I come," she said to the image.

The GPS indicated the shop would be on her right after a few turns—2.5 miles. Sally's Salon was in a residential area. The shop was an addition to a quaint, gray-weathered, cape-style house. The extension sported a sign in the picture window: Hair Color is My Specialty.

"Well, Sally, let's see if your *specialty* can work for me. Only one car. Maybe I'll be lucky and you can take me now."

Parking off the edge of the road, Morgan stepped out of the car, glanced around the tree-lined neighborhood, and sauntered up to the front door of the shop. Pushing the door open a little bell tinkled against the frame, a fortyish, slim, perky woman looked up from the lime-green counter. Her red lips, framed with a flurry of bright red ringlets, turned up into a broad smile. Her blue eyes opened wide under arched penciled brows. "Well, you gave me a start! Saw that blue Olds drive up and I thought Mrs. Thaxter was back to see me. Did you buy her car?"

Panic gripped Morgan's chest … a question … answer it. The woman's bright smile subdued the feeling … a little. "No, I'm renting her house and lucky for me the car is included. Are you Sally?"

"Sure am, hon. What can I do for you this morning? I have a lady under the dryer almost ready for a comb out and then I can take you."

"Perfect. Your sign—color is your specialty. Can you turn me into a blonde?"

"Honey, you came to the right place. Want a new look do you?"

"And a cut. You know what they say about blondes—"

"They absolutely do have more fun. Now you settle yourself in that chair, cubby two, and I'll be right with you. Here's a clip of blonde hair strands. Pick your shade and we'll start the new you in a few minutes. Let me write you in my book. Your name?"

A knot tightened in Morgan's stomach. "Morgan Grant."

"Telephone?"

"I don't know … not connected yet … just moved—"

"Not a problem, hon. New to the area and tons of details to attend to. And, of course, you and I know hair trumps everything else. Now you just sit, pick your color. Here are a couple of style books. Help yourself to coffee. Okay, Mrs. Adams, let's get those curls combed out," Sally said in a loud voice switching off the hairdryer. A gray-haired woman looked up, nodded, and tottered on black sneakers to cubby one.

Leafing through the style book as she fingered the locks of blonde strands, Morgan bookmarked a page and leaned back in the pink vinyl chair. The windows, four panes over four were decorated with lacy café curtains. The shop was charming—lime-green, pink, and white lace, pulled together with large black and white linoleum squares. *A perfect backdrop for Sally and her red hair,* Morgan thought, thankful that Mrs. Thaxter had circled the little salon in the phonebook.

Mrs. Adams soon left and Sally set to work on Morgan. "I love the color you picked—honey blonde. We'll get close today, but you may need a second application to get exactly what you want." After snipping Morgan's strands of auburn to the style in the picture, Sally disappeared behind a curtain, mixed up the honey-blonde color, and returned holding a bowl and a brush in her glove-covered hands. "I love the light-blue sundress you're wearing. The blue will look wicked smart with your new hair color. Here, hon, put those gold hoops in this dish. Oh, those jeweled sandals … luuuvely. They are all the rage right now in York," Sally said as she began sectioning Morgan's hair.

"Is there an ophthalmologist close by? My contact lens—"

"There's a chain off the highway. One of my daughters goes there. I'll get the address for you. Only a mile from here. Everything you need is within what we locals call York Village."

Sally expertly brushed on the thick mixture humming to the Beatles' song, *Let It Be,* playing on the radio.

"Where are you from, Morgan? You don't sound much like people around here."

Stomach knot returned. Morgan's mind went blank, eyes staring back at her from the mirror. "Oh, ah, Wenatchee."

"Wenatchee? Never heard of it. Where's that?"

"Washington. Washington State. Apple country."

"Sounds nice. What brings you to Maine?"

"My parents died … a year ago. We were close. Had to get away."

"Well, hon, if you had a pick of where to live, York is a wonderful place … close to everything. Portsmouth to the south, and then Boston."

Questions. So many questions. What did Zach say …. "And how about you?"

"Me? Oh, I've lived here all my life. Married my childhood sweetheart. We still act like lovers, can you believe it? He's a fisherman."

God, a fisherman? If it wasn't for the globs of goo on her head, Morgan would have run out of the shop. "Does he have his own boat?"

"Heavens, no. He crews on a charter fishing boat. Charter fishing can be iffy, if you know what I mean. The weather plays tricks on us. Anyway, we worked it out that if I did the hair thing we could make it. So he upped and added this little shop of mine to the house. When our two babies came along it was perfect. I could tend to them and still do hair. Had a playpen over there in the corner, high chair, and all the stuff that goes with babies. Now they're nineteen and twenty-one. Girls. Oh my, they are going to be something. Can I get you another magazine? Coffee? I'm going to shampoo and cut Nadine while your color sets up."

"I'm fine, thanks," Morgan said reaching for the two-month old magazine. The two-sink shop was so bright and cheerful, she felt herself relax. Out on her own, her first interaction with a person had gone smoothly, she thought. Not too many hesitations but she had to be quicker with her responses to questions.

After saying goodbye to Nadine, Sally returned, washed and rinsed out the goop from Morgan's hair. The blow dry went quickly as Sally snipped the edges then smoothed the style blowing the strands of hair over the brush, all the while chatting about her daughters.

"There ... how do like that, Miss Morgan Grant?"

Sally twirled the chair so Morgan faced the mirror a smile spreading across her face. "Sally, you're a miracle worker. I'm a new person. I love the style—shoulder length with a soft sweep forward."

"Yup. Short and sassy. Better watch out."

Stomach tightened. "Watch out?"

"Men! They'll be after the new blonde in town," Sally said laughing.

——

PULLING AWAY FROM THE curb Morgan's breathing returned to normal. "The questions. I have to be quicker with my answers. Keep going, Morgan. Eye doctor and the bank. There'll be forms to fill out. Patient record. Bank shouldn't be bad. They always want your money. Right? Right," she said to the blonde in the mirror.

There was a stoplight ahead and a 7-Eleven gas station on the corner. Good. I'll pull in ... casually look around. Buy a coke ... ask about an eye care place ... lost one of my contacts. Ask about a bank. Compare the information with what Sally gave me.

Striding into the convenience store with a studied air of confidence, Morgan purchased the coke and in return gained some useful information from the manager. She intervened when she overheard Morgan's question to the young clerk with a nose ring. The Bank of Maine sounded respectable, and the Family Eye Care Center specializing in contact lenses, according to the manager, was a short distance north on Route 1, within a block of the bank.

With a coke, a smile, and a thanks for your help, Morgan strolled out into the eighty-nine degree air with a spring in her step. I'll go see about a pair of colored lenses first. May have to make an appointment, she said chatting with the blonde in the rearview mirror.

The receptionist at the eye center said there was an open slot in an hour. "Fill out these forms, and then when he's ready to see you you'll be all set," she explained handing a few sheets of paper to Morgan.

Ah, yes. The dreaded forms. Moving to the end of the counter, Morgan glanced at the three people waiting to see the doctor. One woman sat staring at her. No, not at her, through her. No threat there. A young woman was scanning through a magazine and a man looked at her over the top of his newspaper. He smiled. Not in recognition. It was the blonde thing.

Retrieving the information sheet that Zach had prepared from her purse, Morgan began filling out the form. The first page asked the personal questions she had expected: name, address, telephone number, social security, mother and father's name, previous eye doctor, date of last visit, and insurance. Insurance … I'll have to ask Zach.

The rest was straight forward. Space to list other members of the household. Smiling, she penned in NA. The question was not applicable to her. Then a place for hobbies, sports, and did she use a computer? Wear contacts? If so, how many hours per day? Nothing hard to answer. Then came the page for medical history. Well, I don't have a past but I do have a body so I'll answer honestly.

Morgan stepped back to the receptionist and handed her the clipboard. "I just moved to York. Let my insurance drop. I don't think it included eye appointments anyway. I'll get back to you on that. I'll pay cash today."

"No problem. The visit will be eighty dollars plus any glasses, or lenses you order."

Shouldering her bag, Morgan decided to explore the other shops in the strip small. "I'll be back in less than hour for my appointment," Morgan said as she strode out the door and stood in the shade of the building for a few minutes, breathing deep of the warm air. "Well, Morgan that wasn't bad. You handled that quite well. Good for you," she muttered, giving herself a quiet pep talk. She watched the people milling around in the parking lot, at the cars whizzing north and south on Route 1. Nothing sinister. Taking another deep breath, she set out for the Bank of Maine at the far end of the shopping area.

On the way she popped into an electronics store and bought a small digital camera. She'd always wanted one but never thought she had the time.

As she surmised, the form to open a checking and a saving account, as well as a temporary credit and debit card was quick. They were happy to accept the pretty blonde's $1,000 in the checking account and $500 in savings. Nothing but name, address, telephone, and social security number would do for now. Then the woman went into a spiel about their Certificates of Deposit, and the fees that would be charged if she had an overdraft, or the interest charged if she carried a balance on the credit card.

Piece of cake, Morgan thought strolling back for her eye appointment, enjoying the feel of the hot sun on her arms and happy to swap the Florida humidity for the drier air up north. This time her straight back was not an act.

Confidence regained, she smiled at the people she passed, smiled at the motorists, and a man just stepping from his car. An albino.

Morgan froze. Her heart in her throat.

The man smiled, turned, and jogged into the coffee shop, his flip-flops smacking his heels. He was short. White hair was short—a brush cut.

He was not Junior DelaCruz.

Forcing air into her lungs she proceeded slowly to her appointment, her eyes riveted on the entrance to the Family Eye Care Center.

Chapter 6

WAS MORGAN IN TROUBLE? She'd been out on her own for six hours and Zach was beginning to worry. He was sitting on the top front-door step of the little yellow house in his sock feet waiting for her when the blue Oldsmobile swung into the driveway and stopped. She sat looking at him through the windshield. He didn't move. He watched, waited, didn't rush to see if she was okay, deciding it was best to keep his distance. She seemed okay. *Wow, the hair!*

With a sly smile on her face, Morgan retrieved a couple of bundles from the backseat and then walked up the inlaid brick to the front door.

Zach stood, grinning at her. "Looks like you had a successful day, Blondie." If he thought her auburn hair was stunning, the short cut, blonde hair flipping around under her chin, was very sexy.

Dropping her bundles on the walkway she flung her arms around his neck. "I did it."

Sally had rinsed her hair with a strawberry scent and Zach felt a sharp tug in the pit of his stomach. Something he hadn't felt since his thirty-four-year-old wife died suddenly of a heart attack three years ago. Feeling Morgan against him was unnerving. Thankfully she dropped her arms and stepped back.

"Zach, you would have been so proud of me. The whoppers flowed out of my mouth—not at first, but by the time I saw the eye doctor I was definitely a Wenatchee girl from an apple farm. How do you like my hair?" she asked twirling around.

"Very nice."

"And my eyes?" She batted her eyelashes then moved in close so he could see the color. "Which eye do you like best? The one on the right is cappuccino, hazel on the left."

"I don't remember what your eyes were before," he lied. He didn't want to say he'd noticed, but he had. In fact, her violet eyes were the first thing he was aware of sitting across from her in the plane informing her of the rules a witness must follow. Now he remembered the rules a U.S. Marshal had pledged to follow regarding a witness in his care.

"Violet. Definitely had to change that. So, cappuccino or hazel? I think I like the deeper brown, the hazel. They're testers. See the word test?" she asked moving close again, eyes wide.

"I vote for hazel," he said stepping back, picking up her bundles.

"Hazel it is," she replied. "Actually, I ordered the hazel contacts, but if you preferred the cappuccino I would have changed the order. Two pairs are being FedExed. I should have them in two days. So, when I interview with Dr. Farnsworth, I'll be a complete package."

A complete package. Lord, help me, Zach thought. He turned and held the door open for her. "I bought a pizza for dinner instead of Chinese. I wasn't sure what time you'd be home." *Home ... not your home, stupid. Eat and leave before you say something you'll regret. She's talking fast, shoulders tense. Talk to her. Let her unwind. Today was a challenge but she seems to have come through with flying colors. And, why not. She's a surgeon. Must have operated in life and death situations. She'll be fine. She doesn't need a protector—a big brother will do.*

"Pizza's perfect and I'll have a glass of the red wine I saw in the cabinet." Taking the bags from his outstretched hands, she dropped them on the staircase and ambled into the kitchen. "Wow, you did some major grocery shopping," she said looking into the first brown sack.

"I left them for you to put away ... your kitchen."

"Okay. Let's eat our pizza on the deck. Want me to zap it?" she asked spotting the microwave over the stove.

"No, I'll do it. You get your wine. I'll have another beer then I have to leave for Boston."

Morgan looked up sharply. "Oh. I was hoping you would change your mind. Stay for a day or two. Today went well, but I knew you were here waiting for me. I said it went well, but—"

"Let's talk on the deck. You must have questions," he said cutting her off.

A late afternoon breeze stirred the air chasing away the heat of the day. Morgan hadn't said a word as they each helped themselves to a second slice of pizza. Both relaxed, enjoying the quiet of a late summer day, shadows lengthening as the sun dipped behind the tops of the trees.

"I saw an albino man today."

Zach's brows lifted. "And…"

"I thought my heart was going to pop out of my chest. But I gained control, made myself breathe, and then I realized he was shorter, heavier, than … than you know who."

"If you feel someone is watching you, following you, calls you without saying a word, you get in touch with me. You hear?" Zach's legs began twitching up and down, a habit he had tried to tame.

"I hear." Morgan topped off her wine, looked out across the flowerbed, the expanse of grass, the trees, and the birds calling to each other. "It's idyllic here, so peaceful. It's hard to imagine violence on our southern border. Drug smugglers. Drug runners. Men killing opposing men for control. A man killing a competing gang leader in his hospital bed."

"You're doing the right thing, Morgan. Yes, it's peaceful here, and we want to keep it that way."

She ran into the house returning with her cell in hand, index finger brushing across the screen, then a tap.

Zach smiled, retrieving his cell from his pants pocket. "Hello, Marshal Vickers here," he answered in a stern voice, chuckling.

Closing the clamshell case, Morgan sighed, leaned back sipping her wine.

"Tell you what, Ms. Grant. You let me know when those violet eyes turn hazel, and you've dazzled Dr. Farnsworth. I'll come up and take you sightseeing in your new home state. We'll have an early dinner at a little Italian restaurant I know on the ocean before I head back to Boston. You can tell me all about the predicaments you got into and how you weaseled out of them," he said picking up the empty pizza box and beer can, and headed to the kitchen. At the front door he slipped on his shoes.

"Thanks, Zach. Knowing you'll be coming back will help me through the next couple of weeks. I'll call you … for real."

———

Dear Diary.
"No, scratch that."
To whom it may concern ...

Morgan gazed out the window at the beautiful garden in the twilight. Leaning forward, she straightened the pad of paper on her lap.

Scratching out the words, she began again.

If you should find this ...

Her fingers drew a line through the entry.

Dear Mac,
By now you know I'm gone, or worse, believe I'm dead. Maria Grayson did not die, but she is gone for I don't know how long.
Meet Morgan Grant.
I've been told that I must think I'm Morgan Grant or I'm apt to make a slip and he would find me. Of course, you know who I mean.
Morgan had a good day.
I'm blonde now and soon will have brown eyes. You won't recognize me ... if you ever see me again.
From time to time I'll write to you. Already I feel better seeing your name in front of me, drawing my fingers over the letters, imagining that I'm touching you.
I can't mail this letter. But should we meet again, I'll give it to you. You'll know that I was thinking of you.
Your friend, Morgan

Chapter 7

NO SURGICAL TEAM COVERED head to toe in colorful scrubs!

No sterile, brilliant white operating room.

But the thought of seeing patients more than buoyed Morgan's spirits. A few years ago she sat before a medical board of her peers, grilled with questions on what she would do in this or that situation, repeatedly asked for detailed steps in performing a procedure to save a patient's life, so an interview for a position as a nurse did not give her pause.

Nonetheless, she dressed conservatively in a navy-blue suit, skirt at the knee, and a white silk blouse. Taking an appraising look at her image, she was startled at the woman looking back at her from the mirror. Who was she? Blonde hair. Brown eyes. Name: Morgan Grant. She fingered the dainty gold cross with the ruby in the center falling from her neck beneath the folds of the blouse—a gift passed down from her deceased grandmother, a token from her past that she had managed to slip by Agent Donovan.

She stood tall, head held erect, and turned to leave for her interview.

Twelve minutes later she spotted the small tasteful sign hung from a lamppost at the entrance to the driveway: Dr. Richard Farnsworth, Family Physician. Morgan followed the direction of an arrow pointing to parking around in back of the large, white clapboard house.

Morgan's lips drew up. She liked what she saw—friendly, understated, yet professional. Zach told her the doctor had added an office wing to his large Victorian home years ago. Stepping through the entrance, she introduced herself to the gray-haired woman standing behind the window in the reception area. "Hello, I'm Morgan Grant. I have an appointment with Dr. Farnsworth."

The woman's thin lips turned from a smile to a scowl. "Have a seat. Dr. Farnsworth is running late. I'll call you when he's free."

Morgan sighed. "Thank you. I believe Dr. Farnsworth is expecting me. At five. End of the day?" When she didn't receive an answer Morgan smiled sweetly to the woman and took a seat in the empty waiting area.

Within minutes, a jolly silver-haired man with touches of salt and pepper in a white coat, glasses down on his nose, bustled through the door next to the sign-in window. Morgan was instantly drawn to his smiling face thinking him to be a caricature of Santa Claus.

"Ms. Grant, I'm so happy to finally meet you," he said pumping her hand. "Come with me, we have much to talk about. Can you stay for dinner? The wife is anxious to meet you. Please, say you will."

"I'd love to have dinner with you and your wife, Dr. Farnsworth," Morgan replied glancing over his shoulder at the scowling woman behind the window.

"Close up, Harriett. I think we've seen everyone today. You have a lovely evening. We'll start again tomorrow," he said chuckling. "Now, Ms. Grant, you follow me. Don't mind Harriett," he whispered. "She doesn't take kindly to change and there have been many around here the past month."

The next two hours flew by. Dr. Farnsworth asked her to call him Richard unless they were with patients, in which case he liked to be called doctor, he said with a twinkle in his eyes. Morgan responded that first names were nice and she too would like to be referred to as Ms. Grant when in the presence of a patient. There were three examination rooms—one for the current patient, one for the next patient, and the third for the patient preparing to leave.

"Do you always wear a white doctor's coat?" Morgan asked.

"Oh, yes. Martha, that's my wife, thinks it's more professional. Distinguishes me from the patients," he laughed. "I'd like you to wear scrubs. Harriett told me she left six blue scrubs in the closet— freshly laundered. We have a service that picks them up weekly swapping them with a fresh batch. We always wear a fresh one at the start of the day. You're probably wondering if my patients suffer from white-coat syndrome. They don't seem to. These days, with everything so casual, I think they appreciate the effort from their doctor to present utmost professionalism. Don't you agree?" Richard stopped his banter, eyebrows raised as he stood in front of the closet with white coats hanging in a row on one side and blue, yellow-flowered scrubs hanging to the right.

"Oh, yes, I agree," Morgan replied sincerely.

"The same is true for you, my dear—more professional with a uniform appearance."

"Uh, yes, more professional." The flowered scrubs hit Morgan between the eyes. A symbol that she was no longer recognized as a doctor. The symbol of her new life sweeping away what she had worked so hard for. *I'm not going to—*

"Richard, you back there?" a male voice called out.

"Yes, Barly. Come on in. I have someone I'd like you to meet."

"I know you're leaving next week for your fishing trip and I wanted to ask if you have any special instructions—"

The owner of the voice strolled around the corner stopping in his tracks as he approached Dr. Farnsworth and the blonde, hand flying up over his heart feigning love at first sight.

"Who do we have here? Richard, you've been holding out on me. Introduce me so I can ask this beautiful woman to have dinner with me."

"Morgan, don't pay any attention to him. I'd like you to meet Dr. Joe Bartholomew. Dr. Bartholomew is my backup. Joe, this is Ms. Morgan Grant. She'll be stepping into Ann's place until I hire someone permanently. You'll find that Ms. Grant's nurse practitioner credentials are impressive."

"Please, Morgan, call me Barly. And, Richard you would be crazy not to keep this lovely creature around permanently. Now, Ms. Grant, how about dinner so I can tell you how to handle Richard."

Morgan lifted her brows at the brash doctor. "Well, Dr. Joe Bartholomew, I already have a dinner date," she said winking at Richard. "Maybe another time."

"I'm crushed, but I'll definitely turn that maybe into a yes. But Ms. Grant, Morgan, if I may, I'll be looking forward to having you by my side. Richard, when do you leave?"

"I'm heading out on Friday for that little trout stream in New Hampshire I've been telling you about. Martha is going to New Jersey for a month to play nursemaid to our daughter's new baby. Hard to believe, Morgan, I'm a grandfather twice over," Richard explained grinning from ear to ear.

———

SITTING IN THE FOOTED tub filled with bubbles, hot water melting the urge to scream, Morgan reached for her cell and tapped *Zach*.

"Hi, Morgan. I was thinking about you. How—"

"How? I'll tell you *how,* complete with blue scrubs covered with little yellow flowers. I'm trying to stay calm, but it's not working. Zach, get me out of this witness thing. I can't play in Donovan's masquerade. I want—"

"Morgan, please, be patient—"

"Patient … nice choice of words … patience … only a state of mind."

"Morgan, give us time."

"Time seems to be all I have." Morgan snapped her cell shut and, dripping water, reached for the white terrycloth robe hanging on the back of the bathroom door. Curling up on the bed, she pulled the yellow pad and pen out from under the pillow.

———

Dear Mac,

Interviewed with Dr. Farnsworth, Santa Claus, today, for a non-doctor position. Met sourpuss Harriett. And, goody, goody, I get to wear flowered scrubs.

Morgan's life sucks!

Santa's elf, Morgan

Chapter 8

TWO WEEKS ON THE JOB under Farnsworth's watchful eye, Morgan looked forward to the day with confidence and a tingle of anticipation. She was on her own. The doctor had delivered his wife at the airport and he then drove off to meet his friends for the first day of their three-week fishing vacation.

She felt a slight change in the air. September. A new season was on the way. *And I'm on my way,* she thought breathing in the crisp air.

Morgan entered Farnsworth's family practice, ignoring the smile turned upside down on Harriett's face. "Good morning, Harriett. Lovely day, don't you think?"

"Dr. Bartholomew was called to an emergency surgery. I canceled all but routine appointments. Routine prescriptions, refills, and cursory exams remain on the schedule."

Hiding a stab of anger, swallowing a curse word, Morgan asked for a list of those remaining in the appointment book. Putting on the flowered scrubs, she took note of the sheet Harriett gave her. There were eight patients: a mother with a nine-year-old daughter complaining of a sore throat, her excuse for being unable to go to the first day of school; a senior citizen coming in for his six-month checkup, and six others—a *routine* array of patients.

At four o'clock Harriett, her eyes averted as she passed Morgan, escorted the last patient into the examination room. Plucking the patient's folder from the slotted holder next to the door Morgan entered with a cheerful look on her face. "Hello, Ms. Trent. I'm Morgan Grant—helping out Dr. Farnsworth while he's away on vacation."

"This is a pleasant surprise. Don't get me wrong I'm a big fan of Dr. Farnsworth's, been coming to him for years, but it's nice to see a younger doctor for a change. I haven't seen you around. New to our little village?"

"Actually, Stella, I'm a nurse practitioner, temporarily assisting Dr. Bartholomew while Dr. Farnsworth is away. And, yes, I'm new in town. Relocated from Washington State. How are you feeling? Any problems?" Morgan asked scanning the entries from Stella's last visit.

"Knock on wood, I'm pretty healthy. Washington? I spent some time in Seattle. Is that where you're from?"

"No, actually, the eastern side of the state. Wenatchee. Apple country." Smiling, Morgan attached the blood pressure cuff around Stella's arm. Both women remained silent as Morgan took the reading and noted it on the chart. She was now familiar with Farnsworth's system of jotting down information on paper as opposed to entering it directly into the computer. The office was a bit behind the times, something she would talk to Richard about if he decided to keep her on, which at the moment, she was hoping would be the case. Zach said the doctor was desperate to fill the vacancy quickly when the other nurse left so suddenly. Also, Zach indicated Farnsworth wanted to spend less time in the office, start scaling back for retirement—coming in later, leaving earlier.

"Your blood pressure is a bit high, Stella. I see Dr. Farnsworth has you on medication." Morgan said glancing at his last entry. "It was quite high when he wrote the prescription. Looks like it's working, it's down a little," Morgan glanced up at Stella. "Are you having any side effects?"

"No, I really feel good. He likes to monitor me. I think I get worked-up over my job at the office supply store. It's time for my mammogram. I was going to ask him to schedule it for me at the imaging center."

"No problem, I can do that for you." Morgan continued her examination, checking Stella's ears and nose, tapping her knees—reflexes were good. Felt her ankle checking the blood pressure, and asked her to breathe deep while moving the stethoscope over her back.

"I was going to stop off for a cup of coffee after seeing Dr. Farnsworth," Stella said watching Morgan write on her chart. "Seeing's how you're new in town how about joining me? I can give you some tips on where to shop."

Morgan thought for a moment, finishing up her notes on Stella's chart. She saw that they were the same age. Stella went by Ms. and the line for a spouse's name was blank. It would be nice to have a friend and they seem to have connected, so far anyway. "I'd like that, Stella, but then you have to call me Morgan ... out of the office," she added remembering Richard's proclivity to being called Dr. Farnsworth. "Why don't you checkout with Harriett while I clean off my desk."

Stella gave her directions to a little coffee house in a strip mall bordering Route 1 and Memorial Drive, on the east side of I-95. It had been a pleasant day and Morgan could think of nothing better than to end it with a new girlfriend.

Stella was waiting for her out front of The Coffee Bean and together they went inside, both ordering lattes. "I got hooked on these when I was in Seattle," Stella said savoring her first sip.

Morgan raised her cup to her lips just as her cell rang. Checking the caller ID, she smiled at the name—first name only, Barly. She had entered his number in her cell's directory but had only given her number to Harriett in case Dr. Farnsworth needed to get in touch with her when she was out of the house.

"Hello, Dr. Bartholomew, how did you get my number?"

"Lady, I had your number the minute I saw you. Morgan, there's a twenty-car pileup on I-95, one exit south, Kittery. York Hospital put out a call for doctors. I could use your help. Can you meet me at the hospital in five?"

"Certainly," Morgan replied, standing at the same time pulling up the strap of her shoulder bag.

"Meet me at the emergency entrance. I'll have an EMT van ready to take us to the scene."

"Sorry, Stella. Duty calls. Accident on the highway with multiple vehicles. Catch you later." Morgan said stuffing the cell in her pocket.

"Was that the yummy, Dr. Bartholomew? Every woman in York, young and old, will be jealous of you."

Morgan heard the comment as she ran out to the blue Olds. On her way, thanking God that she had scoped out the location of the hospital the day she became a blonde. With one eye on the road, she glanced at her cell to find Farnsworth's cell number she had stored in case of an emergency. She tapped his name. "Richard, there's an accident on I-95, many cars. Barly called for my help. Does the hospital know about me?"

"Oh darn. I completely forgot. I'll call the director and clear it for you. I'll tell the director that Harriett will drop off a copy of your credentials in the morning. Sometime tomorrow stop in to the hospital's HR department. Complete any forms they need. I'll call Harriett. Glad you're on deck."

"The fishing. Any good?"

"Terrific," Farnsworth said chuckling.

"Great. Bye."

Chapter 9

TRAFFIC WAS BACKED UP for over three miles north and south on I-95 as commuters, tourists, and rubberneckers found themselves stalled en route to New Hampshire, Massachusetts or northern Maine and beyond. A tractor-trailer truck had blown a tire, overturned, and the mass of cars and trucks behind, going over the speed limit, slammed into one after the other—no warning, no time to react, no time to stop.

The scene was chaotic. Police cars, fire engines, ambulances, and tow trucks scrambling to get to the victims, horns honking, sirens blaring, and those stalled, in many cases, were yelling. And people. Lots of people. Children crying, bleeding. Men and women triaged as critical, serious, or checked if they were able to walk on their own. Many lay on stretchers as doctors and medics tended to their wounds, then rushing on to the next victim. Others ran to help their fellow travelers, and still more stood by in shock.

Barly handed Morgan a set of scrubs to pull on over her clothes. Truth be told, she was thrilled to be in medical scrubs again. The driver of an EMT van kept the siren blaring as he weaved through the stalled traffic, then onto the grass covered median strip to get to the scene. Maneuvering back onto the shoulder of the road, he pulled the van to a stop by a group of vehicles smashed one into the other. EMT's were giving aid to other groups further down the road assisting in the transport to York's satellite hospital in Kittery.

"I'll start with that truck," Barly yelled racing off. "Follow me."

Morgan started out after Barly but veered away seeing a man hanging out of a red Corvette trying unsuccessfully to extricate himself from the smashed interior. He was bloody, crying out for help.

"Hang on, mister. My name is Morgan. What's your name?" she asked trying to get the man to talk as she knelt down beside him, sticking her head around the mangled door frame. The man's foot was caught under the dash, the edge of the car's hood protruding through the windshield. Blood was streaming from the man's calf. Rooting around in the kit she had been given she found a pair of scissors and quickly cut away his pant leg soaked in blood. "Come on, mister. Stay with me. What's your name?" Morgan asked again as she unbuckled his belt, wrapping it around his thigh for a makeshift tourniquet to stem the blood flow.

The man screamed in pain, and lost consciousness. Morgan shook his shoulder. "Mister. Mister. What's your name? Talk to me," she called out slapping his hand.

His eyes fluttered looking up at her. "Howard Bond. Are you an angel?"

"Stay with me, Mr. Bond. You passed out. You survived a crash."

"Did I say anything?"

"You were out a few seconds—not enough time for a conversation," Morgan said grinning. He had no color but was still alive. "You have a deep gash along your calf. Not life threatening as long as the bleeding stops. Probably slow you down for awhile. Okay, Howard Bond, let's get you to the hospital. I'm afraid your red Corvette did not survive the crash, but you'll be just fine as long as you keep talking to me." Morgan waved at Barly who was giving instructions to the EMT's hiking up a stretcher into their van.

"Barly, over here. Bring a stretcher. His foot is trapped." she yelled.

Barly ran to her, shoved a piece of metal up. "Can you pull his foot free?"

"Yes. I think so," she said extricating his foot as carefully as she could.

Bond screamed in pain losing consciousness for the second time.

Morgan's green scrubs were covered with blood but she waved off another EMT who tried to take her end of the stretcher. She had been on the end of a stretcher holding men bigger than Mr. Bond.

The man opened his eyes, tried to raise his head. "My car. Where's my car? Cell? Briefcase?"

"I'll get them," Morgan told the EMT as he grasped the front of the stretcher from Barly. "Wait for me. Don't leave." Running to the car, she saw the cell on the floor of the passenger side, and the case on the backseat, untouched. Stepping back, she paused, dropped the case, yanked out her cell from under her scrubs and took a picture. She raced back to the van grasping the medic's hand as he swung her inside, slammed the door, and took off.

The case was locked so she stuffed the cell in Bond's shirt pocket. "Mr. Bond, don't worry. Here's your phone and briefcase," Morgan said, setting the case between his arm and the wall of the van. Again with her cell, she snapped a picture of Mr. Bond and his case as he closed his eyes. She'd had an experience in the emergency room during her residency, when a victim died trying to tell anyone who would listen about something left at the scene of an accident. Mr. Bond's case would be put in a safe place in the hospital waiting for him when he asked for it. And in the off chance that someone walked off with it, she had a picture of the owner holding his property.

——

LEAVING HER HAIR SLICKED back from a shower, Morgan pulled on her jeans and padded on bare feet to the kitchen. Five minutes in a microwave, a slab of lasagna piping hot on a plate and a goblet of red wine in hand, she went out on the deck. Setting her dinner and the pad of paper from under her arm on the round table, she smiled at a squirrel with an acorn in its mouth. She knew what she felt earlier in the day was right. Fall was coming. Seeing a cardinal checking the empty birdfeeder, Morgan made a mental note to add birdseed to her grocery list.

Sipping her wine, she leaned back in the chair enjoying the birds, the trees, the flowers and, most of all, her day. Pulling the pen from the pocket of her jeans, she sighed and began to write a letter.

——

Dear Mac,

Whew! Had a big day. There was a terrible pile up, over twenty cars I was told, on I-95. Just think, I-95 runs from Maine to Florida. A life line of sorts holding us together.

I helped an injured man. His red Corvette was totaled. I know I saved his leg … maybe even his life. Don't laugh. Promise? His name is Bond. No, not James. Howard.

This accident really ticked me off. I wanted to do more but couldn't because of my status, or lack of status. Not a surgeon. I'm going to ask Agent Donovan, no, I'm going to tell him and Vickers, I'm signing up to take the Maine Licensing Boards … for a surgeon's license. I have to tell Donovan because he will have to see to it that my so-called records reflect that I fulfilled the necessary internships and residency requirements in … in Washington. I'll let you know what they say. Ugh!

I wonder how you are. Your pops? Did you buy that beautiful charter fishing boat? Of course, the last time I saw it I was terrified that you-know-who had found me. I was terrified you were going to be caught in the middle of my drama.

I wish …

I don't dare wish.

Your friend forever,

Morgan

Chapter 10

THE NEWS REPORTS ROLLED in on television and in newspapers, about the injuries suffered by those involved in the pileup on I-95, as well as the locals feeling real or imaginary aches and pains after hearing about the grim details.

Everyone had a bump, a cut, a sprain, or even a broken bone somewhere in their skeleton. Most required a doctor's attention. A nurse practitioner could handle a cut but not a fracture. As a result, walk-ins crowded the small waiting room hampering those patients with an appointment to be seen as scheduled. Fielding complaints, Harriett called Barly alerting him to the scene in her lobby and asked him to come in early. He replied that he expected the influx and was on his way.

Within the hour, Morgan passed Barly in the hall as he came out of one exam room and she darted into the next. She was surprised to see him but also relieved. "Thanks, it seems we have a different kind of chain reaction today. Did Harriett call you?"

"She didn't ask you?"

"No," Morgan said.

"Darn, and I was hoping you told her to give me a shout. How about a drink after we clear everybody out. By the looks of it, clearing out will be about at the cocktail hour."

"Sounds good." She nodded in the affirmative, picked up the next patient's file in the rack, a new patient, and disappeared into the examination room.

Finally, Harriett took the payment from the last patient and plopped down on her padded swivel chair as the elderly man shuffled out the front door. "Lordy, what a day," she said letting out a breath of air through her thin lips. "I swear I never—"

Morgan looked up as she closed the patient's file. "Harriett, you did the right thing calling in Barly to help. But, if you feel he's needed in the future, I'd appreciate it if you'd check with me first."

"Dr. Farnsworth has always told me to call Dr. Bartholomew if I think it's necessary."

"I understand, and today it was necessary. And, I wouldn't want you to go against Dr. Farnsworth's rules. But, if he's away, as he is today, I want you to check with me first … unless there's an emergency."

"Humph, whatever you say, Ms. Grant. *But* most expected to see a doctor, and Dr. Bartholomew wasn't due for another two hours. May I leave now?"

"Certainly, and, Harriett, thanks for your help. It was very hectic but you shifted the patients around in a very orderly fashion."

"Didn't take a lunch break, not that you'd notice."

"Oh, I noticed, and I appreciate your staying to see to the patients."

Retrieving her purse from the drawer under the counter, Harriett stood to leave. "Goodbye, Dr. Bartholomew. Thanks for answering my call." With a nod to Morgan, Harriett strode out the front door like a general who had prevailed in battle, her nose a tad higher than normal.

Morgan turned catching Barly leaning against the wall, arms crossed over his chest chuckling at the sparring match between the two women. "I doubt Richard has ever dressed down Harriett. Too afraid she'd leave him."

"Well, she did the right thing calling you … and I too thank you for coming so quickly. She seems to have taken a dislike for me and she'd better get over it. I like team work. I appreciate her taking initiative, but she deliberately went behind my back. There wasn't anything I couldn't handle."

"How about that kid's broken arm?"

Morgan kept her mouth shut. She'd said enough in her present capacity.

Barly grinned. "I think the lady could *handle* a glass of wine or maybe something stronger like—"

"A double martini with two olives. You drive, I'll follow."

"Yes, ma'am. Let's do it. In case you lose sight of me, there's a bar, the Antlers, perfect for this situation … guaranteed to hook you. Noisy, but not too rowdy."

"Antlers?"

"You're in moose country, baby."

Chapter 11

HAPPY HOUR WAS IN full swing at the Antlers Sports Bar and Grill. Three television screens kept up with the latest in hard news and the latest on the New England Patriots football team, along with interview after interview with victims of yesterday's I-95 collisions. Selections from the jukeboxes, mounted on the wall of every booth, provided a counter balance of rock-n-roll to the drone of the television reports as the patrons fed quarters into the slots.

Barly raised his stemmed glass, two stuffed olives staring up from the bottom of both martinis. "Here's to a good day on the field of battle."

"Cheers," she responded taking a sip. Eyes closed, she let the vodka slide down her throat. "Mmmm, the Antlers' bartender mixes a mighty fine drink. Just what the doctor ordered," she said with a hint of a laugh.

"I have to say, Ms. Grant, you surprised me yesterday. When I asked you to assist me, without hesitation, you went in the opposite direction and took care of Howard Bond, silencing his usual diatribe."

"Diatribe?"

"Yeah. He's known around here. In fact, if he wasn't laid up with that gash in his leg, he'd probably be out somewhere shooting off his mouth about the poor downtrodden citizens in our country."

"Wow, I wouldn't have expected that—downtrodden? With a red Corvette?"

"He's a day-trader by day, activist by night and weekends. He was probably setting up a trade and took his eyes off the road when he crashed. As I said, you surprised me. You're tough. Know what needs to be done and you do it."

"Tell me about your practice, Barly." *How's that for a smooth redirect,* she thought, grinning inside.

"Formed a clinic with three other doctors after completing my residency. We're all from around here—York, Kittery, Ogunquit. We saw a need for one-stop shopping: cardio, neuro, psych, and peds."

"Men? Women?"

"All men except for pediatrics."

"And your specialty?" Morgan asked nodding to the waitress in thanks for the small bowl of mixed nuts she set on the table.

"Cardio—diagnosing, care, and surgery. We're affiliated with York Hospital. They provide top-notch OR surgical teams."

"Are you the only doctor providing backup for Richard?" Morgan began to realize there was more to Dr. Bartholomew than she thought at first. *Snap judgments are not always right, can be misleading. Maybe the playboy attitude hides someone else, a deeper man.*

"Yes, but we all fill in when needed. Richard is an institution around here. A woman wouldn't think of taking her child to anyone but Dr. Farnsworth. Then, if he refers them, they will come to us … even after all these years. Hard to believe we opened our doors six years ago. How about you? How would your patient history read?"

Morgan stabbed the last olive in her glass and Barly signaled the waitress for another round. He leaned back, wondered what the beautiful nurse sitting across from him was going to say. This was unusual for him. He never cared what a woman had to say as long as she agreed to spend the night with him, or a weekend up north in a cottage he had built on Moosehead Lake. At least that was his fantasy. He was well aware of his reputation, a womanizer. Because he didn't correct what was said, the gossip confirmed it as fact.

He looked into the warm brown eyes that stared back at him waiting, wanting to hear her story.

"Well, let's see. I was an Army brat. No siblings. My dad served several stints in Alabama, hence, I'm told, I have a slight southern accent. When he deployed outside the US, mom liked Alabama so we stayed there. When my father retired early, they returned to their roots—Wenatchee, Washington. That's where I was born. He couldn't sit still, bought a few acres and became an apple farmer. They both died in a car accident. I had to get away … make a change. Through a colleague I found that Dr. Farnsworth was looking for help, and I thought the opposite side of the country would be about right. And there you have it, my patient file."

Barly wanted to take hold of her delicate fingers circling the stem of her cocktail glass. Normally, in his fantasy, he would have done so, and would have asked the pretty woman to accompany him to his house. He'd cook up a batch of pasta, and then, after a bottle of Chianti, escort her to his bedroom. But no fantasy this time. Not this woman. She was different and he didn't want to jeopardize seeing her again. "So, you ran away." *Strange,* he thought, *she has an air of confidence about her, wouldn't run from anything, but there is also something very vulnerable behind those eyes.*

Barly wouldn't have believed it if someone told him the woman sitting across from him, her eyes suddenly filled with pain … apprehension … held a secret she wanted to tell …

"What about you, Barly. What are you running from? I'm thinking you're hiding behind a playboy image?"

Chapter 12

WHO IS THIS WOMAN?

She certainly speaks her mind.

Barly sipped his drink, his forearms resting on the table, his eyes scanning Morgan's face. Whoever she was, she had him pegged. He drew away from the warm brown eyes, feeling they were looking into his soul. Impossible. Must be the alcohol. He wasn't ready. Ready? You're getting ahead of yourself, my boy. "What makes you think I'm not a rascal?" he asked.

"Your actions yesterday at the accident. You weren't the only one observing. Of course, I have it on good authority that all the women in this village called York are after the yummy Dr. Joe Bartholomew. But that's it. No tales of wild conquests, only the chase."

Barly shook his head, stifling a laugh, a smile playing on his lips. "So that's the word is it?" He looked up. "All the women in York village?"

"That's what I was told," Morgan said shifting her legs, waiting for his version of the chase.

"There was a woman, but not from here."

Morgan's brows arched. "I thought you grew up here?"

"Yes, but my residency was elsewhere … New York Presbyterian Hospital's Center for Cardiovascular Health, lower Manhattan."

"Very impressive. Couldn't have been much time for extracurricular activities there. NY Pres. is rated number one, if memory serves me correctly."

Barly swirled his martini in the stemmed glass. "Your memory serves you."

"What happened there, Barly?"

"I met her. Julie. She was a cardio patient. I was assigned to her. I killed her." Barly spoke staring into his glass, his mind visualizing a woman on the operating table.

Morgan reached across the table, laid her hand over his, held tight. "Barly, residency is tough. We see things, experience things, things that are out of our control. We shouldn't, but sometimes we blame ourselves."

"We?"

"You saw things. I'm sure you didn't cause her death? Was she more than a patient to you?"

Morgan continued to grip his hand as he ran his thumb over her smooth skin.

"She'd been on the cardio floor, in and out, for over a year. During good times, when she was released from the hospital, we began seeing each other. It was wrong. But, I don't think it clouded my judgment, still, I knew it was wrong. I had assisted in several open-heart surgeries. Twice I was given the lead under the supervision of a brilliant surgeon.

"This night, Julie was admitted around 2 a.m. She had suffered a massive heart attack. I was the only cardio doctor on duty. I began the surgery. The doctor I had assisted many times was on his way. He didn't make it. She died on the table." Barly closed his eyes. Shook his head but the image of Julie lying on the table, the monitor's droning sound, remained. He withdrew his hand from Morgan's grip, sighed and downed his drink, signaling the waitress for another.

"So, Ms. Grant, that's my story. No one before Julie, except a couple of trysts in the room set aside for doctors to catch a few zzzs when pulling a double shift, and no one after."

———

DAY HAD TURNED TO NIGHT. Morgan kicked her shoes off and flopped down on the bed. Stretching out, she ruminated over the day and drinks with Barly. He certainly had opened up to her. She began to feel their mutual heartache—he losing his lover on an operating table, and she … well Morgan had made the choice to leave Mac. She saw it as leaving him, but also trying to save him, keep him from becoming entangled in the danger surrounding her.

Turning over, she fished under the pillow and pulled out the pen and yellow pad of paper.

———

Dear Mac,

I almost blew my cover today. It was wild at the practice—yesterday's accident victims and regulars. The day ended with my having some harsh words with Harriett. She doesn't like me in her territory and I don't approve of her being so territorial. Of course, what really got under my skin was the fact that she was right. After all, she is in charge of the office and not the nurse, meaning yours truly.

The backup doctor, while Dr. F. is on vaca, escorted me to a bar to dampen the steam coming from my ears. Yes, steam. It worked.

I also learned that Dr. Bartholomew isn't the playboy he's reported to be. I have to say it felt good to talk doctor to doctor. Naturally, that was from my perspective of the conversation. Because of my situation I have to be careful of what I say, but I think Dr. B. can be counted as a new friend.

I wonder how you are. Out in the Gulf? Showing a group the fine art of sport fishing?

Good night, my dear friend,
Morgan

Chapter 13

HOWARD BOND WAS PISSED OFF. Nothing had gone his way the past couple of weeks. Ever since he wrecked his beloved red Corvette everything he touched turned sour. The shipment of guns he was expecting had been delayed. His customer, a militia group in New Hampshire, threatened to buy elsewhere if Howie didn't deliver.

Howie didn't want to change his source because the man told him of a new product he would be selling soon—marijuana—the best he had ever seen. But yesterday, the source had canceled their appointment.

Bad news.

Howie liked to light up at the end of day, ease the tension in his neck and back from the hours he spent bent over his computer, watching the stream of quotes passing in front of him, buying stocks on their dips, and selling when he felt they had gained the most he could expect. Yeah, it would be nice if he could light up on someone else's dime, if he could slip out some, sell the balance to someone else to cover his cost.

Rolling a couple of weeds every few hours also helped to release his anger as he watched the late-night news. He hated the government—all the regulations that had come about because of the financial meltdown. How was a man to make any money?

He was delighted on the day when he met like-minded souls in a bar. The men had formed a militia and were arming themselves, a body of citizen soldiers defending their individual rights. Their stories sealed the deal for Howard Bond. He was one of them. Joined their cause. Would help their cause, and if he profited in the deal so much the better.

This morning started worse than the morning before, when his printer jammed documenting his numerous trades. And now to make matters even worse, a stabbing pain was shooting through his leg. All thanks to a clumsy intern at the York Hospital who tripped over a stool, landing on his leg, resulting in the popping of several stitches. Screaming out in pain, he cursed that he'd had enough of the hospital and its staff. No more follow-up appointments in York, he'd find his own doctor where he lived, in Portsmouth.

No, it had not been a good morning on top of his other problems.

At the moment, he had to figure out how to hold the door open of the office supply store, navigating with a crutch under each arm.

"Howie Bond, fancy you coming into the shop. Here, let me hold that door for you."

Howard, scowling, looked at the perky brunette. He didn't recognize her, but she at least had the courtesy to come to his rescue so she couldn't be all bad.

Catching his black trousers on the handle of a cart by the front door, she caught him as he stumbled forward losing one of the crutches, his usually slicked back brown hair falling over one eye. Laughing, she put her arm around him guiding him to a chair, removing her arm as he flopped down. "Okay, Howie. Sit here. Tell me what you want and I'll get it for you. Does your leg hurt?"

"Throbbing like the devil," he said smoothing his hair back.

Seeing the distress he was in, Stella had another thought. "Better yet, switch to this desk chair with wheels. You can scoot around the aisles with me. I'll do the reaching while we chat … telling me what you want."

"Am I supposed to know you?" Howie asked, feeling better that someone seemed to care that he was incapacitated and in pain.

"Senior year. York High School. You were the nerd in calculus sitting in front of me. A class I flunked. I must say you don't look nerdy now. I'm Stella Trent. Well, I was Stella Higgins. I'm divorced—Mr. Trent left a few years back for God knows where, so if you want to thank me with a drink after we get your supplies you can. That is, if you want to."

"Ah … sure. A drink sounds like a good idea. I do remember you, Stella. Not the Higgins or the Trent names, of course." He didn't remember any of the girls in high school having the delightful scent of … what was it? Lavender? Of course, the soap his mother swore by, buying out the local Walgreen's drugstore where they lived.

Fumbling in his pocket, again dropping a crutch on the floor as he switched chairs, he pulled out a folded sheet of paper, shook it out and handed it to the smiling Stella Trent.

His day had taken a decided turn for the better. The fact that she had definite curves under the lavender sheath she was wearing was also a plus.

Chapter 14

A MONTH HAD WHIZZED by since Morgan arrived in York. It wasn't that she didn't feel safe, just a little uneasy, glancing over her shoulder at times to see if she was being followed. *No death threats,* she thought chiding the frowning woman in the mirror. *Face it, you jump at every sound. You need someone to protect you and don't even think of asking Zach to station a policeman. He wouldn't anyway. Said I was on my own. If not a guard ... how about a guard dog? Morgan, you've never even had a bird as a pet. Leave a dog home alone all day? Maybe a cat? Oh sure, a Bengal Tiger but not a tabby. Would Richard tolerate an arrangement ... let me bring a dog to the practice? Yards fenced ... partially.* "Can't hurt to ask," she said barging out of the employee restroom.

"Hey, watch where you're going young lady," Richard said laughing.

"You're back," Morgan said, catching his extended hand to keep her balance. "Have fun?"

"Yes, and yes. The fellas and I had a marvelous time—men stuff, out in the woods, stalking our prey, cooking over a fire. Ah course, some nights there were only scrambled eggs for dinner. Talked to Martha. Not sure when I can pry her away from our grandbaby. Another week at least. Tell me what's spinning in that head of yours. I know from Martha that if she walks into something there's something on her mind."

"Nothing really. Not true. What would you say if I got a dog ... bring it to work ... the fence—"

"Wonderful idea. The wife and I had a dog. Big Shepherd—Bonnie. She died of old age and we never replaced her. Didn't want the responsibility, you know—feeding, walking."

"You're right. Maybe I should rethink—"

"Nonsense, a dog is a capital idea, but don't tell Harriett. She's not a dog person."

"Great. Something else to dislike about me."

"She doesn't dislike you, Morgan. Harriett has a difficult time with change. Now, you'll have to tell me later about what happened while I was cooking up those batches of trout ... that big accident on I-95."

Heard? Who told him that? Barly, of course. No, I called him about the hospital. Did they have my records?

In between patients, Morgan called the local Humane Society inquiring if they had a rescue dog. Not a puppy. An older dog. A trained older dog and must be exceptionally good with adults. When the woman on the phone heard Morgan was working with Dr. Farnsworth, she said she might have the perfect dog. A real sweetheart.

———

COME ON, JENNY, let's meet your new family," Morgan whispered knocking softly on Richard's open door. "Ahem. I have someone I'd like you to meet, Doctor."

Richard looked up from the pile of patient folders on his desk. "Well, well—"

"This is Jenny. Jenny, shake hands with Dr. Farnsworth."

"Would you look at her. How do you do, Jenny. A Golden Retriever. You're a real beauty, Jenny," Richard said shaking the dog's raised paw swiping the air for the human's hand. "And so respectful."

"She's a rescue dog. Four years old and knows all the necessary commands plus one, maybe more I don't know about yet, don't you, Jenny. Lay down, Jenny. Good girl," Morgan said pulling a little biscuit from her slacks pocket. "Roll over. Nice, dog. Sit," the proud parent commanded, giving her new dog another biscuit.

"Why would anybody give up a dog like this?" Richard asked, scratching Jenny's ears.

"Moved away ... into an apartment I was told."

"What's the plus one?"

"Jenny! Teeth!"

Jenny spread her lips, along with a menacing growl. "My, my. Very fierce, but I swear she's grinning at me. Let me have that leash, Morgan. Okay, Jenny, come with me. Let's go meet Harriett."

Jenny trotted beside Richard, looking back at Morgan for her okay.

Hearing someone coming down the hall, Harriett twisted her desk chair around and spotted the furry face with a pink tongue hanging out coming her way.

"Harriett, I'd like you to meet Jenny. She's our new mascot. Shake hands with Harriett, Jenny."

Jenny trotted up to Harriett who was pushing her chair back, hands in the air against an emanate attack. Jenny, thinking the new human was ready to play, barked ever so softly, sat, and thumped her paw on Harriett's knee demanding to shake hands.

"Oh. Oh. Nice doggie. Now, go away."

Jenny was going nowhere until the human shook her paw.

"Shoo."

Jenny slapped her paw on Harriett's knee again and then gently placed her muzzle on her lap, looking up with big brown eyes, and a crooning sound asking to be friends.

"I said, shoo," Harriett ordered, but softer this time giving Jenny a tentative pat on her silky head.

Satisfied with the pat, Jenny turned and sat next to Richard. After all he had the leash in his hand.

Standing in back of Richard, Morgan watched wide-eyed at the scene playing out over his shoulder. She soon learned that Jenny, the wonder dog, had won over Harriett, something she had failed to do.

The next morning, when Morgan passed Harriett's desk taking Jenny to the fenced area in the backyard, there was a plastic container of wipes on her desk. Jenny dutifully pulled to a stop, sat, waiting for a pat. "Oh, all right. I suppose you are a nice dog. Here, Harriett has something for you as long as you're going to be our mascot." Harriett opened her bottom drawer fetching a biscuit from a medium-sized box. Jenny's nose followed her action and delicately accepted the morsel, being very mindful not to touch the two fingers holding the treat.

Chapter 15

IT WAS THE STUPIDEST idea Zach had ever heard. Just because the Feds couldn't find Junior DelaCruz that was no reason to put Morgan out there as bait. Sitting in the chair, his heel clicking on the floor in frustration, he waited in the Field Office conference room for Morgan. Zach turned, his eyes shooting daggers at Donovan.

"You can't be serious—a decoy? More like a sitting duck," Zach said springing to his feet.

Agent Alex Donovan was dead serious. "We can't find him. The trail is ice cold. Junior DelaCruz has abandoned his house, his villa, whatever you want to call it. He took everything and everyone with him. Our undercover agents in Mexico are grilling their contacts. No leads. Vanished. And yet there's evidence that the DelaCruz cartel continues to operate—Texas, Arizona, Louisiana, and Florida. Another border guard was killed last night."

"Hold off, Alex. Morgan is due here any minute. Don't you dare say anything to her about your cockamamie idea until you and I discuss it further."

Both men looked up at the soft knock on the private conference room door as Morgan stepped in. "Hi, Zach. Hello, Agent Donovan. Long time no see," she said extending her hand. Her steely exterior belied the knot in her stomach, a reaction whenever she met with Donovan. She presented an image of a confident woman. Dressed in a navy blue suit, and heels, her white silk blouse open at the throat but not enough to reveal the gold cross on a chain around her neck. The hint of gardenia followed her into the room.

Zach had arranged the meeting at the field office at Donovan's requested. The agent needed more from his witness, a witness that could help convict DelaCruz of murder if they couldn't get him on gun running or drug trafficking. It took years to convict Manuel Noriega. That case came to trial and ended in a conviction in 1992—

eight counts of drug trafficking, racketeering, and money laundering.

If Donovan and the agents assigned to this case couldn't convict DelaCruz on drug trafficking or gun running, then murder would be just fine. And, God forbid, if something should happen to Morgan Grant, AKA Maria Grayson, Agent Donovan wanted her testimony on videotape.

"You sure look different, Morgan. The hair. The eyes. I doubt your own mother would recognize you," Donovan said.

When Morgan's eyebrows arched in surprise that he would say such a thing, he realized, too late, the insensitivity of his statement. Her mother, suffering from Alzheimer's, rarely recognized her daughter before, let alone now.

"How is my mother?" Morgan asked sliding onto the chair Zach had pulled away from the table for her.

"I spoke to the director at Sunrise House this morning," Donovan replied.

"How did you represent yourself?" Morgan asked.

"Same as always ...an officer for your estate. A polite inquiry that funds were being dispersed, as you had willed, from an executor who had taken over your mother's estate because of her inability to handle her own affairs. Bottom line, she rarely has a lucid moment, but on the good side seems fairly content. She continues to mumble about two men—Danny and Artie."

Morgan looked down at her hands folded in front of her. "I see. I guess that is good. Agent Donovan, can we get on with this ... the questioning?"

Donovan sighed as he ambled to the electronic whiteboard mounted on the front wall of the conference room, a room without windows, a room swept for bugs before every meeting. What went on in this room stayed in this room. Turning to Morgan, he said, "If it's all right with you, we're going to videotape our session?"

"Okay."

Behind a sliding door at the opposite end of the room was a video camera connected to a computer ready to capture a lecture, a status report, or, in this case, a witness's testimony.

"Before you begin, Morgan, I'm going to give you a recap of where we are in the case. The list of players, at least those we know to date. As we learn more, Zach or I will update the board. Anything written on it will be saved to a computer file so we can call it up at any time in our office, or on our laptop."

Donovan pushed a button and the board instantly displayed a computer file, information that Donovan kept current in his office and had sent to the Boston Field Office.

Case: DelaCruz Cartel	
Target: Junior DelaCruz, missing	**Believed he killed:**
Crime: Murder, Gun Running, Drugs	√Perez
Last seen: Anna Maria Island, FL, 3 months ago	Studs
	Wally

Morgan leaned forward, following Donovan's dissertation as he pointed to the names on the board.

"With your testimony, we know Junior murdered Arturo Perez." Donovan entered a checkmark next to Perez. "We believe that he tried to scare you off by ramming your boat, returned to Cortez, and killed Studs and Wally making it look like a murder suicide. We have evidence showing Wally and Junior together, proving they knew each other. We think Wally was Junior's lieutenant, a clumsy lieutenant, and had become a liability." Tapping the keypad at the bottom right of the board, a picture of Wallace Gutfeld appeared.

Morgan stood, walked to the board. "I've seen this man. I don't remember ... yes, in the hallway of the Manatee Memorial hospital. A lawyer for the hospital ... he was questioning me. This man walked by, dropped something, looked at me strangely, and then ... must have walked on down the hall."

Donovan glanced at Zach. This was exactly what he hoped might happen. That Morgan had more information stored in that beautiful head of hers, and Donovan wanted to mine every last nugget.

"Good, Morgan. As for Studs, the Cortez police came up with his real name: Ricardo Torres."

"Studs crewed for Mac." Morgan said sighing. Mac's name was not on the board as a person of interest.

Donovan narrowed his eyes. *Ah, the fisherman.* "You haven't been in touch with Macintyre have you?"

"No, Agent Donovan, I haven't."

"As I said, we found a connection between Studs and Wally. They were seen together a few times in Cortez. We think Wally recruited Studs for the cartel's drug operation, but we can't prove it other than some residue in an ashtray in Studs' room that he rented, the room where the two were found … murdered. Unfortunately, these three dead guys can't tell us where Junior is. We can't find him."

Donovan tapped a key clearing the board. "So, now you know what we know, Morgan." He walked to the other end of the room, slid open the door, and turned on the camcorder. "Zach, please put a chair for Morgan at the end of the table. And now, Morgan it's your turn."

Testifying as to what she saw, Donovan interspersed questions from time to time. She reiterated what she witnessed in the hospital room, witness to the albino, she had since learned was Junior DelaCruz, turning off the equipment that had been keeping Arturo Perez alive. She learned that Arturo Perez was a man Junior had grown to despise, a man who murdered to steal business that rightfully belonged to the DelaCruz cartel. A man DelaCruz killed, thereby removing the brains of the rival cartel.

When Donovan turned off the recorder Morgan stood, paced to the front of the room at the same time taking a deep breath. There was no point in putting it off any longer, and besides she had just given them something they wanted, so it was only fair that she ask for something in return.

"I'm going to take the Maine Licensing Boards … for a surgeon's license. Please see to it that my so-called records reflect that I fulfilled the necessary internships and residency requirements in … in Washington."

The agent and the marshal exchanged glances. Donovan looked back at Morgan. "Let me see what I can do. I'll let you know."

———

WALKING OUT OF THE field office with Zach, Morgan inhaled the fresh air, cleansing her body and mind of the memories Agent Donavan wanted to capture on the camcorder, memories Morgan wanted to leave behind.

"Donovan seemed upset when I first walked into the conference room. Anything to do with me?"

"Yes, he was out of sorts. Not with you. With the case. Seems his agents can't locate Junior DelaCruz. The last known sight of him was yours—the boat he tried to ram you with, and then walking up the path to your house when you called Donovan for help."

"What's he going to do … to find him?"

"He and his agents are going to keep searching. It's not your problem, Morgan."

Chapter 16

ELIZABETH STITCHWAY GRASPED HER fiancé's hand as they walked along the busy array of shops, restaurants, and outdoor cafés in Boston's Quincy Market. "I'm so glad we came to the conference. Aren't you?" The vivacious redhead looked up at her fiancé, a former Daytona Beach Police Captain and now her business partner. Because it was a business conference of sorts, they chose to wear their personal PI uniforms: black shirt, trousers, and shoes.

They legally formed their partnership shortly before they were engaged: Private Investigators for Hire. They had worked together prior to their incorporation—she a PI, he a police captain. But when Manny left the DB Police Department they joined forces—personal as well as business. He wanted to get away from all the regulations and ever increasing paperwork to allow him the freedom to delve into the realm of private investigation.

Elizabeth planned to keep her maiden name as far as their business was concerned. She had developed a following as a PI, but on paper, as of the end of January, she would be Mrs. Elizabeth Stitchway Salinas.

Manny looked into his fiancée's eyes. "I love you, Stitch, and yes, I'm glad we came to Boston."

"Wasn't Rudy Giuliani inspiring? And the real-life episodes that NYPD's Commissioner Ray Kelly related were scaryyy. Things we have to watch out for, be aware of in our area of Florida. We're ripe for that militia stuff."

"How about a cup of coffee at that little café?" Manny asked. "We can do some people watching."

"Good idea, Sherlock."

As was their custom, they chose a little spot where they could observe without being observed. The waitress brought their order—coffee black for Manny and a latte laced with vanilla flavoring for

Liz. They sat quietly exchanging an occasional observation of this and that.

Stitch closed her eyes, sniffing the air. "Manny, can you smell it?"

"What," he asked smiling.

"Oh, I don't know—grilled sausage, chocolate cake, hot pretzels … and our coffee," she said taking a long sip.

A couple sat down at the table next to the investigators, backs turned to them. The man asked the blonde a question. She responded with a soft laugh.

"Manny!" Stitch whispered sitting up ramrod straight.

"What?" Manny caught the alarm in Liz's voice.

"Did you hear that?"

"Hear what?"

"That woman's laugh. I've heard that before. Don't look."

"Stitch, you're getting a bit carried away—too much terrorist stuff we heard about today."

"Manny, the woman … her profile … Manny, it's Maria."

"What?" Manny started to turn his head to see but Liz grabbed his arm.

"Don't look! Let's listen."

"I can't hear anything."

"Neither can I. They're whispering."

"What are you doing?" Manny asked watching Liz pull her business card out of her shoulder bag.

"We're leaving. You're going to hand my card to the waitress as we go. Ask her to give it to that blonde while I take a picture with my phone. When we get up, we go out through the other side of the café."

"What are you writing?"

Liz handed him the card so he could read her note: "You look wonderful. My lips are sealed. Call if you need help. Liz."

———

A WAITRESS SET TWO fish sandwich orders in front of her patrons. Pausing, she pulled a card from the pocket of her black apron and handed it to the blonde. "Is there anything else I can get for you two?"

"Morgan, do you want an iced tea refill?"

Morgan's eyes darted around, searching the people chatting at the various tables. "Where is the woman who gave you this card?" she asked the waitress, in a controlled voice. "I don't see her."

"I don't know. It was a man. He was with a woman. I think they left. I'll get you both more tea," she added in a pleasant voice.

"Morgan, whose card is it?" Zach asked taking the card that she held out to him. "Do you know this Liz?"

"Yes, and she definitely ID'd me. She's a friend … was a friend. She and her fiancé are private investigators in Florida. He had a contact, an officer in Texas. He was the one who came up with the name of Junior DelaCruz, before I called Donovan. Did you see a redhead sitting in back of us?"

"No, but I'm afraid I wasn't looking. We were talking. Let's go. Walk!" Zach said, slapping some bills on the table. Sauntering out of the café, they merged with the throngs of people enjoying a warm October afternoon.

"I have to report this to the department but I think you're okay. It was bound to happen sooner or later," he said quietly taking her hand. "Remember what I told you. If you see someone from your past, turn the other way and leave quickly."

Morgan looked him square in the eyes. "Zach I wasn't the one who saw someone. Someone saw ME. Even with the changes to how I look, she made me."

"Yes, but she doesn't know your name. She saw you in Boston not in York. Your cover was not breached. It's okay, Morgan."

Zach propelled her through the crowd milling about in the Market. Doubling back, he escorted her to her car, gave her a long hug, and waved goodbye as she drove out of the parking garage.

Watching her car disappear down the ramp, Zach jammed his hands in his trouser pockets. Maybe Donovan is right. The case is going nowhere. We need a break and Morgan is the most likely person to flush DelaCruz out of hiding.

Chapter 17

Sierra Madre Mountains
Western Mexico

JUNIOR RAN HIS FINGERS ALONG the soft suede of the wide-brimmed felt hat covering his clipped white hair, shading his sensitive pink eyes. Black shirt and trousers, gloves, boots and neckerchief covered the rest of his pallid, sallow-skinned body. At five-foot-five, he was not a formidable man physically. He carried some extra weight due to his staying indoors out of the sun, never in the fields working the crops. He wasn't feared only for his physical characteristics, but more for his reputation as a ruthless leader, demanding servitude from his men or they simply vanished.

But Junior also had a fear. He desired the love of a woman, to have children, but feared the albino gene would be passed down to a baby. He saw a doctor, had surgery, becoming incapable of fathering a child. He made plans to marry soon. He had picked a mother for his child and would see to it that she was impregnated believing it was his sperm the doctor planted. Then he would claim the child as his. There were ways to get what he wanted, and he always found them.

His ultimate joy was riding his stallion through the hills, over his land, always affording him supreme control over his life and fortune. Today was one of those days. Giving a yell to Devil, the black stallion took off up the steep terrain.

Junior DelaCruz was joined by his new lieutenant, Felix Mendoza, a head taller than his leader, stocky with ripples of hard muscles—his arms, his trunk, his legs. He was a handsome Mexican with inky black hair, mustache, artistically clipped goatee framing his deep olive skin. The two men were riding the hills on the pretext of checking the new crop of marijuana. Junior was eager for a private conversation, eager to hear every word of what Mendoza gleaned from his research into the death of Dr. Maria Grayson. Was she really burned alive when her car rolled over in a Florida ravine?

Loose ends.

Junior hated loose ends. He didn't suffer dim-witted people very long. He had eliminated his former lieutenant, Wallace Gutfeld, and the womanizer Wally had unwisely hired—Studs. Junior never did find out what his real name was and didn't care. The pair was no longer a menace to his operation. Besides, Wally, brainless as he was, knew too much about the border activities of the DelaCruz cartel and Junior's plans to take over all operations in the southern Border States of the U.S.

Junior loved riding through valley after valley of the rugged, pine-covered region where the air was crisp and free of pollutants. *Yes, times are good,* Junior thought. *I won't allow anyone to disturb my cannabis crops growing in these mountains.*

Marijuana, the cannabis weed, was Junior's cash cow, taking only a few months for the crop to mature into ten-foot tall plants. The Mexican army's eradication squads that thrilled in hacking down the illicit fields had been diverted by the drug war raging elsewhere in the country.

Junior kept his business on a tight leash, drawing on cross-border criminal networks to deliver the cannabis to scores of U.S. cities. It was a dangerous business. Smugglers working for the DelaCruz family were known to have been killed for losing a load of marijuana. A couple of pounds of marijuana sold locally for barely $15 to $20. But when the weed moved closer to the U.S. border the price climbed.

Once the product was smuggled into the States, such as Arizona and Texas, the price soared above $500 a pound wholesale. Before he died, Junior's father could smuggle several tons of marijuana hidden in tractor-trailers that were crossing the border. With new methods of detection, the cartel now smuggled the weed through tunnels, ultra-light aircraft and even packing it on the backs of illegals trying to cross the border.

Junior had recently set up a farm in southern California, negating the need to cross the border. He employed illegal migrants to guard and maintain the hidden site.

Cannabis was the cartel's main source of income but Junior had diversified into weapons, especially various guns which were becoming increasingly difficult to purchase in the U.S. but easy to obtain on the black market.

No, Junior wasn't going to take any chances on being caught, ending up rotting for years in an American jail cell. All because a woman thought she saw him turn the ventilator off of a man, Arturo Perez, recuperating from heart surgery, a man who led the operations of a competing cartel. The man Junior had promised his father, laying on his deathbed, that he would eliminate.

The ride had been invigorating, but it was time to rein in Devil, to discuss with his lieutenant how he wanted a certain situation to be handled.

Tethering their mounts to a nearby tree, Junior and Felix began their inspection of the current crop of cannabis as Junior began his orders.

"Felix, I've told you about Dr. Maria Grayson. I know her mother suffers from advanced Alzheimer's, and that she is being cared for in a home, Sunrise House, in New Orleans. If Dr. Grayson is alive, I believe there is a good chance that the dutiful daughter will try to contact her mother."

"Sí, I understand where you're going, Señor. You wish me to see to it that if Dr. Grayson does inquire about her mother, or better yet, actually speaks with her on the phone, you would like not only to know the contact was made, but more important, proof that the doctor is alive. Am I right?"

"You always know my thoughts, Felix. I would like you to use whatever method you deem will give you this proof, and to do this immediately after you check our crops in California. By the way, is the cannabis thriving?"

"Sí, Señor, San Diego is a perfect location. The crops are growing like *weeds* in the crevices of the Palomar Mountain range," Felix said chuckling.

"Excellent news. It is so much easier to transport the *weed* from within the U.S. eliminating the problems of border crossings. I have ordered my plane to be checked and ready for you to fly to San Diego and then on to New Orleans so you can attend to your new assignment. Hmm, I think there is one addition to your assignment, another stop after New Orleans."

"What is that, Señor?"

"There is a fisherman. He lives in a little fishing village in Florida. Cortez. He and Dr. Grayson were becoming romantically involved from what Wally had told me. It would be wise for you to apply the same surveillance techniques as you use with Dr. Grayson's mother."

"What is this fisherman's name?"

"Charles Macintyre, but he's known as Mac."

Chapter 18

New Orleans, Louisiana

A WHITE VAN DREW up in front of Sunrise House, a private senior-living home for women afflicted with Alzheimer's. A forty something man dressed in a black suit, white shirt, and black tie exited the vehicle. Reaching into the backseat he retrieved a gray leather-bound notebook.

The manager of the facility, chatting with a staff member, noticed the van and the man through the parlor's picture window and proceeded to the front door to answer the doorbell.

When the manager opened the door inquiring what she could do for the man, he hustled by her flashing his credentials.

"Are you Mrs. Trebly," he asked as he glanced around.

"Yes, sir, but—"

"Not to worry, ma'am. The Louisiana Board of Health and Services is conducting unannounced inspections of all senior-living centers. We've had some complaints about unauthorized drugs being administered to patients in their care as well as, shall we say, rough treatment. I've been authorized to take a walk-through of your facility, ask a few questions, and then I'll be on my way. It looks like you provide a wholesome environment. My records show you added a wing on the back of the house to provide six private rooms. Is that correct?"

"Yes, but—"

"Good. Now, if you would please give me a list of your residents and their room numbers, I'll then proceed with my required walk-through."

Mrs. Trebly didn't want any trouble with the State. It was hard enough keeping up with all the regulations, so she quickly retrieved the list of residents noting their room number beside each name. As she handed the list to the man, an aide hustled to her side telling her that Mrs. Scott had soiled her bed sheets. Mrs. Trebly hurried down the hall with the aide. The inspector followed to room number one and entered, leaving Trebly and the aide to attend to Mrs. Scott in room five.

The elderly woman in room number one sat staring at the television. The room was bright and clean with a decided rose fragrance. She looked up as the inspector entered the room. He smiled at her, glanced around, checked off her name, nodded, and left.

He entered room two occupied by a Mrs. Grayson sitting in a chair, her head down, eyes closed, snoring softly. The inspector stepped to the nightstand and examined the telephone, then the dresser. He checked off her name, and quickly popped in and out of the remaining rooms.

The manager was smoothing a clean sheet on Mrs. Scott's bed when the inspector poked his head in for the second time. "I'll be leaving now, Mrs. Trebly. Thank you for your help. My report will show that you have a well-run facility. Have a nice day."

The man stopped briefly at the vacant front desk, lifted the receiver on the desk phone and then replaced it. He strode out the front door, returned to his van, and drove off down the tree-lined street.

Chapter 19

Cortez, Florida

LOVERS HOLDING HANDS, Manny and Liz strolled down the dock eager to join Mac and his pops for a day of fishing. They were a pair all right, down to the black trousers, black T's and shoes. While Manny had been out on the Patty Sue, joining other sports fishermen on the Macintyre and Son Sports Fishing Charter, it was the first time Liz had come along.

"Remember, Sherlock, don't let on you've seen Maria."

"I'm still not convinced that blonde was Maria, but, whoever she was, she hasn't called."

"Sherlock. Look at *that* blonde with her arms around Mac's neck. That sure isn't Maria and he isn't exactly pushing this blonde away. Maybe your fishing buddy has moved on," Liz said.

"I met her before," Manny said. "She was on one of the fishing excursions Mac asked me to join."

"How did he introduce her—*the new love of my life*?"

"No. Her name is Florence Patterson. She's a realtor in Cortez … they have an arrangement. She refers newcomers who are interested in fishing to him, and he refers his clients chartering a day of fishing if they mention an interest in moving to the area, to her. Lots of building going on in Cortez. Tourists visit, see how beautiful it is and want a piece of the quaint fishing village."

"Well, it looks like they're thinking of making the arrangement permanent, if you know what I mean. They haven't budged an inch to come up for air. And, would you look at those high-wedge shoes. He's going to have to lift her up to the dock."

"I hear you, but I didn't get that inference from Mac. Of course, it's been several weeks since I've seen him … still, that's hard to believe. He is … was … really in love with Maria. Maybe he's beginning to believe the story that she was killed in that car crash.

We'll find out soon enough," Manny said returning Mac's wave. "Hey, Mac, good to see you. I feel lucky today—maybe an Amberjack?" Manny called out giving Liz a hand as she jumped from the dock to the deck of the Patty Sue.

"Flo, you met Manny and this is Liz, his fiancée," Mac said with a chuckle.

"You've got that right, Mac," Liz said giving him a hug. "Nice to meet you, Flo. Are you joining us today?"

"No—"

"Flo just came down to tell me about her prospective new client."

"Felix Mendoza. Luuuvs fishing so I steered him to Mac." Flo's big blue eyes gazed up at Mac, and then her ruby lips pecked his cheek. "You guys have fun. I have to run. Have to take care of my agency, you know. Oh, would you look at that. Here comes Felix now and a couple I haven't seen before. Did he call you, Mac?"

"Last night and the couple chatting with him must be the Lamberts. Honeymooners. I don't know about his bride, but when he called he sounded like an avid fisherman. They drove down from Atlanta for the week. Here comes Pops. He's been charting a new course on the maps in the cabin. Careful, Liz, he's liable to put you in a hammer lock. His eyes lit up when I told him you and Manny were coming with us today."

"Elizabeth, my star pupil," Danny said hugging Liz and then shaking Manny's hand. "Let me help these other folks aboard, and then I think we can head out, son."

Mac helped Flo up to the dock and then welcomed Felix and then the Lamberts, all were dressed in jeans, white T-shirts, and sneakers. No jackets. Mac always carried several yellow slickers in case of rain or a cold wind especially with the advent of fall. He quickly passed them off to his pops to get them situated with rods, reels, bait, and some basic instructions for Mrs. Lambert. She laughingly cut the instructions short. She and her new husband were avid fishermen.

Felix thanked Danny for the rod and moseyed to a deck chair near the starboard side away from the others. Liz joined Mrs. Lambert and they quickly fell into a conversation about weddings.

Mac, Manny in his wake, climbed to the flying bridge to get today's fishing excursion underway, Mac at the helm, Manny sitting beside him enjoying the view from the bridge. The two men struck up where they left off the last time Manny went out on the Patty Sue. Manny asked how the fish were biting, how the charter business was doing and then inquired about Flo.

"Oh, Flo and I … mostly business and not funny business. By the way, I don't know if you've stayed in touch with the officers here, you know the double murder—Studs and the guy they call Wally. The police found a partial print on Wally's gun that didn't match Wally or Studs, but no hits on the Fed's database."

"No, I haven't talked to them. So it goes in the cold-case file?" Manny asked.

"Whatever you cop guys call it," Mac said checking the course Pops had drawn.

———

DANNY, HIS HOST CHORES done for the moment, sat next to Liz. They both put their shoes up on the rail, Liz her head back enjoying the sunshine.

"Danny, is it serious between Mac and Flo?"

"I hope not. I keep telling him to watch out. Flo has all the mannerisms of Regina. Don't get me wrong, Regina did right by me. Gave me Mac after all. But when Patty Sue left me at the altar, at least I thought that was the case, until I found that letter from Perez confessing he had given her some pills that killed her. Of course, he said it was an accidental overdose, and I tend to believe a dying man's letter. Anyway Regina didn't waste a minute. Swept me away from the church, and before I knew it we were making a baby that night on the beach. Darndest thing.

"Trouble is I see the same thing happening to Mac. What is it they say, déjà vue? I know he's carrying a torch for Maria. Has a broken heart losing her. He's hurting. I catch him when we're out at sea staring at the water. Makes me want to cry. But, it is what it is. Maria's gone and Flo's here wangling her way into his heart, or maybe taking advantage of the situation. I think she's in love with

Mac. I know he's lonely and Flo's arms are mighty inviting. I know how that works on a man."

"It's so sad," Liz said.

"You know, Elizabeth, maybe I was wrong a minute ago when I said I hoped Mac wasn't serious. Maybe he should take up with Flo … seriously."

——

MENDOZA REELED IN HIS LINE, checked his bait, added a fresh piece of herring and let the line out again. His back was to Danny and the Elizabeth woman. *So, the fisherman is still pining for Maria. But, from the gist of the conversation, she obviously hasn't been in communication with him. As the pops fella said, Mac thinks she's dead. Still, Junior can't take any chances.*

"Hey, Danny, do you have a phone on the Patty Sue or a ship-to-shore radio? I have to call my boss and I forgot my cell," Felix asked over his shoulder.

"Sure. Go in the cabin. Can't miss it. Help yourself," Danny said without moving, enjoying Elizabeth's company.

A few minutes later Mendoza strolled back on the stern, stroked his goatee, sighed and prepared his line for more fishing. He was having a great time. Hell, he felt good. His assignment in Cortez was a complete success. Staking out the fisherman's house earlier in the day, he planted a bug in Macintyre's home phone. And a second just now in the cabin phone.

Yes, Felix loved fishing. It was always a good day when he could mix business with pleasure. Grinning, bait on the hook, he swung the rod back and then snapped it out over the water. It was a helluva good cast.

Chapter 20

York, Maine

THE BLACK SUV CRUISED north on Route 1, a bit under the speed limit, skirting the Atlantic Ocean. Zach wasn't in a hurry, wishing the day would last forever. Morgan twisted in the passenger's seat to face him, her seatbelt tightening across her ribs, outlining her figure under the little black dress. Her soft scent of spring violets, and the seatbelt, left little to his imagination, as if his mind needed any help. He had put off making this trip to York until the need to see her overwhelmed his better judgment. *I'm just doing my job. Making sure my witness is okay,* he thought. *Oh yeah, just keep lying to yourself,* countered the voice in his head.

Morgan stared at him, waiting for him to speak.

Turning, he sighed, a smile playing around his lips. "What?" He quickly looked back to the road.

She squared herself in the seat loosening the seatbelt so she could breathe easier. "Just waiting for you to tell me what Donavan has on his mind."

"Donavan?"

"Yes, he called this morning. Said you had an update for me."

"Oh. It can wait. Talk to me ... how are things are going? You and Farnsworth hitting it off okay?"

"He's very nice and so is his wife. I told you they went their separate ways a few weeks back—he fishing with his buddies, and she went to help their daughter with a new baby."

"We didn't get much of a chance to talk when we met in Boston ... that business card thing. How did it go ... on your own when Farnsworth went fishing?"

"Fine. Richard's backup on call, Dr. Joe Bartholomew, a cardiologist, helped out. There was a pileup on I-95. It was awful.

We worked together along with the EMTs transporting the injured to the hospital. Barly was great."

"Barly?"

"That's what everybody calls him. There was this guy—drove a red Corvette, but no longer. It was totaled. You'll never guess his name."

"Which is?"

"Bond," she laughed, her soft musical notes. "He had a terrible gash on his leg. Zach, I hate to say it, but it was good to have blood on my hands again. I applied a tourniquet to stem the blood flow. Barly said I did a good job."

"Because you knew how to apply a tourniquet?"

"No, how I handled myself at the scene. The man screaming in pain … bleeding. Remember, I'm a nurse. I surprised him, I guess, because I went off on my own. Didn't follow him. And, I have a dog. You didn't meet Jenny when you picked me up because she was with Harriett, Richard's office manager. Runs the place. Hates dogs but Jenny won her over. That's my dog."

"Sounds to me like you're settling in quite nicely," Zach said as he pulled into the last spot in the small parking lot.

"Mimmos? What kind of a name is that?" Morgan asked unbuckling her seatbelt, leaning forward to read the sign.

"Italian. One of the best Italian restaurants on the Maine seaboard. One drawback—they don't offer wine with the meal but happily will serve ours. So, young lady, we are going to walk up the street and buy us an outstanding bottle of red wine."

———

WAVES CRASHED AGAINST THE rocky shoreline. A storm, miles out at sea, coupled with the incoming tide, was a perfect backdrop for the restaurant. Patrons, safe inside, were enjoying the power of Mother Nature on the outside of the window, the glass framed with white tie-back curtains.

The hostess led them to a window table overlooking the ocean across the highway and the large boulders serving as a retaining wall against the onslaught of the waves. However, some waves ran over the road escaping the barrier.

Morgan's mind filled with Mac's image, his fishing boat, and the waters of the Gulf. What was she doing sitting here, looking out at another body of water with another man, who she could tell thought of her more than just his witness.

"Morgan. Morgan," Zach said softly, touching her hand resting on the white tablecloth.

"What? Sorry, you were saying."

"I said, it sounds as if you are adapting well to your new life. In Maine."

"I guess so." Morgan continued to gaze at the ocean. The tide continued to rise spewing water laced with salt crystals high in the air. There was an outcropping, cutting the beach in half with the high tide. She felt the waves crashing on her chest, her life cut in half by the miles of land between herself and Mac.

Zach closed his hand over hers. "It's okay to miss the people in your old life. It will get easier."

Morgan turned to him. "Will it? I wonder." Pain was in her eyes. The chatty woman in the car turned wistful in the candlelight. An Italian tenor sang an aria floating from speakers tucked into the rough hewn ceiling beams. It should have been magical, perfect for lovers, but Mac was miles away.

"Zach, it's not natural to suddenly be cut off from everything you know, especially from people who are close to you. If you move away because of a job opportunity, you still maintain contact with loved ones and family. You can visit. They can visit. But this ... Zach, I have to establish a date, a date to be released from your care. I'm not going to be a witness that Donovan described as staying in protection for good, no, staying in this new *life* is what he meant. I'm going back. Maybe not tomorrow, or next month, but ... before the end of next year."

Morgan swiped at a tear before it hit her cheek. Turning her eyes from Zach, she watched a swell building far out in the water, racing to shore, then smashing against the boulders. Feeling the strength of the swell, Morgan lifted her head, held her breath letting it escape slowly. "Yes, I have to go back."

The wine Zach purchased up the street had been poured, their order of veal and pasta enjoyed, and the after dinner coffee served. Zach hadn't commented on her ultimatum, choosing to turn the conversation to amusing antics of their childhood.

Morgan sipped the espresso in the candlelight warming the atmosphere, windows now a mirror against the black night. A mirror reflecting a couple who seemed to be enjoying each other's company. The man's bald head and horn-rimmed glasses catching the flicker of the candle, his white shirt unbuttoned at the neck, looked like he belonged with the lovely blonde sitting across the table.

"My mother … how is she? Have you checked lately? How did you identify yourself? Has she asked for me?"

"I called yesterday afternoon so I could give you the latest," Zach said. "I spoke with a Mrs. Trebly—"

"She's the manager. She's nice. What did she say? Did you talk to my mother?"

"No, I didn't talk to your mother. I guess she was sleeping. When I call I say that I'm the lawyer for her estate. Same thing Donovan says, that I'm verifying that Sunrise House received the latest check, asking if there is anything your mother needs. Trebly said that your mother had an occasional touch of reality and might mention her daughter's name, but, more often than not, rambled on about a man called Artie."

"Artie. Arturo Perez. She's still fixated on him. They may have been lovers. Small world. Perez, the man I saw DelaCruz murder. I didn't know until later that Perez had sent a letter to Daniel Macintyre, Mac's father, confessing that he was the one who gave Danny's bride the drugs that killed her."

"Yes, I've read the story. Very tragic."

"Tragic indeed. And then his son is left alone by another tragedy—a car crash burning up his lover." Morgan spit out the words in a whisper. "It's not fair, Zach. I'm going back!"

"Well, that's what Donovan wanted me to talk to you about. The Feds still can't find DelaCruz. The Feds can't get anyone to flip, give him up, or give us some intel on where he is. They think he's still in Mexico."

"So, what's Donovan's message?"

"He has a plan, an idea—leaking information that maybe the doctor, who saw him murder his arch rival in his hospital bed, didn't die in that car crash after all. That she's alive and well—"

"Bait! He wants to use me as bait because his people are too incompetent to find the kingpin of a major drug cartel. Is that it?" she whispered, words filled with anger.

"Yes, but—"

"No yes-buts, Marshal Vickers. You tell him my answer is no deal. Next thing I know Jenny and I will be hiding out under the trapdoor I found in my house, the room I use for my computer."

"Where does it go? Stairs?" Zach asked with a chuckle.

"There's a small basement under part of the house with a bulkhead door from the outside. When I asked the realtor about the door, she said the Thaxter's had the door built in ... it's under a small throw rug. They used it at times in the winter if there was a problem with the gas furnace. It's more of a cellar than a basement."

Zach had delivered Donovan's message. Dinner was over.

Leaving the restaurant, they stepped into the starry night. The sound of the waves crashing ashore seemed ominous. Zach's jaw tightened. Muscles from years of training as a U.S. Marshal tightened. He casually rested his arm around her shoulders as they strolled to the car. It was a protective gesture. Protection against what he feared was ahead for his witness, a witness he wanted to protect for a life with him, a desire he continued to struggle against since meeting Morgan Grant.

———

Dear Mac,

Had dinner with Zach. You won't believe the message he delivered to me. Agent Donovan wants to use me as bait. The Feds can't find DelaCruz so he thinks I can draw him out. I said no.

I told Zach to give Donovan my ultimatum. He has until the end of next year. If he hasn't wrapped up the case by then, I'm coming home, back to Florida. I'm coming back to you. Of course, that's irrational. I'd be putting both of us back in danger again. But, that's what I dream of doing.

I miss you,
With love,
Morgan

Chapter 21

A SOFT CHIME ANNOUNCED the man's arrival at the office supply store. A bluster of mid-November air pushed him in as he swung through on his orthopedic boot. Stella Trent circled the checkout counter to assist the lone customer with the door, her eyes bright. Finally he had returned.

"Howard Bond, my, my, you seem to be doing well since I saw you last. How's the leg? Here, let me get you a chair." Stella's black dress sprinkled with tiny white polka dots clung to her figure, falling in soft gores from her waist, flirting with her knees as she walked. Puckering her dark red lips together to even the color, she bedazzled him with a pretty smile.

"I'm fine, thanks for asking, Stella. One more week and I can throw this boot away. Here's a list of stuff I need—mainly a couple of flash drives. Always afraid I'll lose a file," he replied with a wide smile.

The dress, the long brunette waves circling Stella's shoulders, and the red lips seemed to have had an impact. Pleased with his reaction, Stella plunged on reminding him of her words the last time he came to the store. "I wish you'd take me up on my offer, Howie. I could do many things for you, make it easier for you, so you don't have to get up. Hobble around. Hey, it's almost closing. Want to have a drink down at the Whippoorwill? I promised I'd have a drink with you. Remember?"

"Stel, that's a capital idea. The markets are closed so no more trading today, and I'm scheduled to meet Paul Thaxter at that bar in a little while."

"Wonderful. Give me a few minutes to fill your order. I'll drive you, hon. Only down the end of the strip, but I wouldn't want you to trip with that boot."

With Howie's order processed, Stella put on her coat and turned down the thermostat. Locking the door, she stashed the bags in the back of his car. Howard navigated to the front seat of her car, pulling his foot in as Stella closed the door.

At the Whippoorwill, Scottie nodded from behind the bar at the pair as they entered. He called out to Howard. "Vodka, ice on the side?"

"You got it. And the same for Stel."

Stella settled in a private booth toward the back as Howie, fumbling with his jacket, fell into the booth chuckling that he'd be glad to be rid of the darn walking cast.

Scottie strode up with their drink order and bowl of pretzels. "Give a wave if you want something else."

Stella leaned over grasping Howard's free hand. "Are you sure you're all right, hon?"

"Sure am, sweetie," he said smiling over his glass. "Cheers."

"How's the market doing for you, Howie? You said you were trading today."

"And a hell of a day it was. So bad I have to confess I had a drink before shutting down the computer. Honest to God, go figure, up one day down the next. Hell, up one minute down the next. Stel, this is great … seeing you. How about we have dinner? Can you do that? Have dinner with me?"

"Howie, I'd love to but I thought you said you were meeting Paul Thaxter."

Stella's heart flipped in her chest as she smoothed the skirt of her dress. Howie seemed to be interested in her, calling her sweetie and all. Practically insisted they have a drink and now dinner. She didn't know if she should play hard to get or easy. She did know she was eager to be gotten.

He was so darn good looking and he had to have money, scads of money. Putting his purchases on the seat of his car, she smelled the newness of the leather. The new Corvette replacing the one that was totaled in the accident was black with a creamy interior. She'd like to sit there … next to him.

She looked up feeling his eyes on her, warm eyes. The fluttering of her heart instantly shot to her belly.

"It'll be a quick conversation. He owes me an update on an order I placed with him."

Stella tried to think, concentrate on what he was saying, but his eyes were all over her.

"My, my, you are busy. Can't imagine what Paul, a military guy, would sell to you."

"Nothing you need to worry that pretty little head of yours about, sweetie."

Pretty little head, oh God. Stella was saved, given time to compose herself when Paul Thaxter strolled up to the booth.

"Geez, could you find a darker place," Paul said. "Didn't see you until Scottie pointed back here. Hi, Stella."

"Nice to see you, Paul. How's your mother?" Stella said, her heart returning to a normal beat.

"That's where I'm going next and then to the homestead. Want to check out the new tenant, a Ms. Grant. See how she's doing."

"I've had coffee with her a few times—very nice and *very* pretty. Blonde. I bet you'll find everything in order. Give my best to your mom when you see her."

"Don't hang around on our account," Howie said.

Stella glanced from Paul to Howie. She sensed a slight irritation in Howie's voice. *He wants to be alone with me,* she thought, her heart flipping.

"Stel and I were about to order dinner. Just tell me when my stuff is coming. The guys are getting antsy."

Thaxter looked at Stella, then back at Howie. Raising his brows, he nodded slightly toward Stella. He wasn't sure he wanted to talk in front of her.

"It's okay, Paul. Just tell me the date."

"I'm having some trouble … with the dealer. But it shouldn't be more than a couple of weeks."

"Dammit, Thaxter. You said the same thing last week. Maybe I'll take my business somewhere else."

"Now, Howie, don't twist your knickers in a knot. I said I'm working on it. I'll be in touch. Bye, Stella. You get prettier every day. Maybe you and I … next time."

"Oh no, you don't," Howie snapped. "Now get out of here and don't forget I'll be expecting your call one week from today or else."

"Yeah, yeah." Thaxter winked at Stella and sauntered out of the bar.

Stella sat dumbfounded, her blue eyes wide at what just happened—two men obviously quarreling over her. At least that's how she saw it. But best of all, wonders of wonders, Howard Bond indicated she was his girl.

"Stel, I've been thinking about what you said back at the store … about helping me. I have several irons in the fire, so to speak, and could use some help … part time to start, mind you. Maybe after dinner we get my car and I follow you to your place. We could talk about it."

Chapter 22

THE BRILLIANT COLORS OF fall were fading fast, leaves blanketing the earth in the crisp air of late November. Barly kept his eyes on the road for the short jaunt to the Stage Neck Inn, built on a bluff overlooking York Harbor. It was a favorite spot of his and he was anxious to show Morgan the view of the sandy beaches tucked between the rugged outcropping of rocks along the shoreline.

His eyes were on the road but his hand covered hers resting on the leather seat of his black Mercedes. He felt good. No, he felt great, smiling as he turned down the hill to the inn. It was a beautiful evening. Maybe they could take a walk on the beach after dinner. No, it would be too cold. But … maybe.

The maître-d smiled as one of his favorite people walked in, the handsome man with salt and pepper hair impeccably dressed in a dark gray suit, white shirt, no tie—casual, understated. Tonight he strolled in with a beautiful blonde on his arm. A stunner in a white dress leaving no doubt about the curves outlined under the soft fabric. "I'm glad you called, Dr. Bartholomew. Your table is waiting, the one in the window overlooking the harbor, as you requested."

The little man led the way as if the emperor was following in his footsteps. Barly had performed emergency heart surgery on the man's wife a year ago, saving her life. Guests glanced up as the handsome couple passed in the soft glow of the candles, white tablecloths, and sparkling stemmed glassware.

Their waiter, Carl, replaced the maître-d and stood at attention to receive the doctor's drink order.

"We'll have two manhattans?" Barly looked at Morgan for her okay. She nodded in agreement, and Barly added an order of crab cakes. "Oysters?"

Nodding yes, she turned back to the view of the rocky shoreline of York Harbor.

"… and two servings of your oysters. Thanks, Carl."

The doctor's personal waiter returned quickly with the drinks, the appetizers to follow in a few minutes.

"Barly ... the ocean, the rocks ... the view. And to think it's only, what, ten minutes from Farnsworth's practice and your special group," she said.

Barly tapped his glass to hers. "To more spectacular views. I've only begun to show you around. Wait until we go to my cottage on Moosehead Lake, up in Greenville. Strap on a pair of cross-country skis, the boards—"

"Boards? In my case, that would have to mean splints," Morgan said laughing.

Barly loved her laugh. It was soft, musical, her brown eyes sparkling with merriment.

Over dinner of grilled salmon and swordfish, he entertained her with stories of encounters he and his partners had with patients since he put together the practice.

The sun slipped away for the day, replaced by a full moon sending slivers of light over the spectacular view below the bluff, the crashing waves pounding to reach high tide. Barly watched her. She was suddenly somewhere else, a wistful place ... a touch of sadness around her eyes.

After Carl set their order of espressos on the table Barly reached for her hand. "What is it, Morgan? You look sad. What do you see with those brown eyes?"

Her lashes slowly slid down ... lingered a moment then popped up. "Nothing ... it's lovely here—"

Barly looked down, retrieving his vibrating cell on his belt. "Which road has the best access? ... I'll be there in fifteen with a nurse. Have scrubs ready for us and a pair of sneakers for the nurse—anything over size six."

"What is it," Morgan asked setting her napkin on the table.

"The Down-easter train jumped the tracks, or the rails were tampered with. They're not sure. There are fatalities."

As he spoke he took her hand leading her out of the dining room. "An emergency, Carl. Put the bill on my tab. I'll swing by tomorrow to take care of it," Barly said whizzing by the startled waiter. The pretty blonde matched the doctor's stride step for step.

Chapter 23

THE MASSIVE ENGINE OF the train lay on its side against an embankment, each car behind skewed at a different angle with the last in line remaining upright on the track. The landscape appeared like the opening scene in a horror movie. Acrid smoke filled the air from several cars catching fire on impact, or was it due to a bomb? Sirens from additional medical vans blared, mixing with the horns of fire engines, mixing with more sirens from squad cars disgorging police officers trying to bring order out of chaos.

Rounding a bend to the crash site, eerily lit in the bright lights of the rescue vehicles, Barly slammed on the brakes of his car, stopping beside an EMT van. Barly and Morgan didn't hesitate jumping out of the car, racing to join the medical teams. The driver from the York Hospital medics handed them scrubs and a pair of sneakers to Morgan as she threw her high heels to the side. Sneakers laced, she ran to join Barly who was yelling to a York EMT. "Where do you need us? Where should we start first?"

"The triage. To your left. They're still removing victims from the cars."

The first medics on the scene had set up triage areas, separating critical victims from those who couldn't walk, and from those who could be checked and released. Stretchers and blankets were lined up on tarps spread out on the grassy land bordering the tracks. The stench of smoke swirled around the victims, forming plumes in the air from the windows and from underneath two coach cars lying on their side. The cars were scorched on the outside, some gutted by fire on the inside.

Darkness hampered all their efforts as teams ran with flashlights searching for the injured and in some cases the dead.

Morgan glanced up as she helped an elderly man to a blanket, catching a glimpse of Barly nearby helping a woman who was going into premature labor. He motioned to her, needing her help.

Morgan took over for him as he attended to the woman's young son screaming in pain, his arm dangling unnaturally from his shoulder. The mother, now lying on a stretcher, tears rolling down her cheeks, was picked up by a medical team and taken to an ambulance as Barly tied a makeshift splint around her son's arm, gave him a shot for the pain, and then carried him to the ambulance to be transported to the hospital with his mother.

Barly heard Morgan calling for a tracheotomy kit, asking the EMT to assist, to hold the flashlight. Without a second's hesitation, she performed the procedure on the man dying from a collapsed lung. She then ran alongside the stretcher taping the tube protruding from his throat to his chest as another attendant ran up with a portable oxygen tank.

Shocked momentarily by Morgan's action, Barly turned to a fiftyish man crying out in pain, his pants stained with blood.

ATF authorities arrived scouring the train, the tracks, the surrounding area for the cause of what they were beginning to believe was an explosion. The wreckage was a grizzly backdrop to the chaos of the medical teams, stretchers and ambulances leaving, only to return for more victims. Many were taken to sister hospitals in the towns of Kittery and Ogunquit. Other officers methodically went through the debris searching for more victims who moments before the derailment were returning from a holiday in the north country of Maine, a pastoral, sometimes rugged, retreat.

The last of the critical victims were lifted into an EMT van, an ambulance, or the backseats of cars. The last bus pulled off the grassy field to the road, transporting those who didn't require medical help.

Barly caught up with Morgan, grabbed her arm. Both were bloody, faces smeared with dirt. "What the hell did you think you were doing back there?"

Her brows squeezed together trying to understand what he was asking.

"The trach," Barly said staring at her.

"He was dying. There was no time … I didn't see you. I had assisted once—"

"No time to discuss it now. Can you come to the hospital? They paged me. They're overwhelmed."

"Of course. Let's go."

Barly grasped her hand as they stumbled in the dark following the beam of his flashlight to his car.

"I probably won't see you after we're in the hospital," Barly said spinning the tires on the damp grass, the car lurching onto the asphalt road. "Let's talk in the morning … probably won't be until afternoon. I'll call."

Morgan flopped back against the headrest. Her eyes closed. She wondered if they would let her help with the surgeries.

Of course not, not yet anyway.

An hour passed. Barly didn't know what Morgan was dealing with as he cracked the chest of a seventy-two-year-old man in cardiac arrest. They had been sent in different directions once they reached the hospital.

Morgan stripped off the bloody scrubs, throwing them in the bin, noting that her white dress was ruined, stained with blood that managed to seep around the covering. She was immediately handed a fresh set and ushered into a flood-lit, sterile operating room to assist a surgeon facing a woman with a nearly severed leg. The surgeon quickly determined that there was no way the leg could be saved.

———

Dear Mac,

Too tired! You know that cliché—bone tired? Now I know what that means. There was a train wreck—so many victims.

Later.

Morgan

Chapter 24

WITH A NUDGE OF a cold nose and a slurp on the cheek, Jenny insisted it was time to let her outside. Morgan patted her companion on her golden head.

"Okay, girl. As they say, 'up and at 'em.'"

A dusting of snow had fallen in the three hours since Morgan had left the hospital, a dusting that would melt in the morning sun. The events of the prior evening slowly crept into her brain: dinner with Barly, and the train wreck. She had made a difference.

"I saved a man's life last night, Jenny. You should have seen Barly's face. No one said anything at the hospital about my performing a tracheotomy. There wasn't time. Hopefully, I'll slide by under their radar."

Morgan let Jenny out to frolic in the snow, chase the squirrels, and do her business while Morgan showered.

Thanks to the slurp on the cheek, she made it to work on time. Morgan poked her head into Farnsworth's office to wish him a good morning, receiving a half wave in reply. A scowl on his face, he didn't look up from his computer. Jenny picked up her treat from Harriett, and then flopped down by Morgan's desk.

Farnsworth retrieved the email he printed, showed it to Harriett, and then called Morgan into his office. Nodding to her to take a seat as he skirted his desk and, with a sigh, sat looking over his glasses at her. "Must have been quite a scene—train on its side. I saw you a couple of times at the hospital, passing in the hall. Not much sleep I imagine. I know I didn't get much."

"Will we have a lot of walk-ins? Last time, the pile-up on I-95, there—"

He cut her off. "An email just came in … from the hospital … the director."

Richard was definitely in a surly mood. She waited to hear if the message had to do with her and the emergency surgery she performed, the trach.

He handed her the email.

It was short stating that she had performed a procedure, a procedure which she was not licensed to perform. She was hereby reprimanded, and, if she overstepped her position again, she would not be welcome at the hospital and would be reported to the Maine Health and Services Department, who could revoke her license. She was lucky this time that the patient didn't die.

Morgan leaned forward and laid the piece of paper on Farnsworth's desk.

"She forgot to mention that I saved the man's life," Morgan said her words dripping with sarcasm. Remembering her *position*, she leaned back in the chair. "I'm sorry, Richard, but I would do it again. If someone is dying and I can help, I will do everything in my power to save him."

"That's just it, Morgan. This was not in your power. Whatever possessed you?"

"I … I assisted a surgeon before. I knew what to do. There was no one else. All the doctors were tending to other victims. If that's not part of your Hippocratic Oath, then fire me."

Richard stared at her, his eyes tired, his body fatigued.

"Now, if you'll excuse me, I have to prep the patients for you to examine." Morgan felt like storming out but she didn't. It wasn't Richard's fault. He didn't know that she had performed the same procedure more times than she could count. She walked out, pulled on the flowered nurse's scrubs, and stepped into the first examination room with a smile on her face to take the woman's blood pressure.

Harriett overheard their sharp words. She stepped into Richard's office closing the door behind her. Richard's face told her everything. He was torn with how to handle the situation with his nurse.

"What's your opinion of Morgan?" he asked softly. "You've worked side by side for almost four months."

"She's very competent. Certainly seems to know what she's talking about—deeper than a nurse, more like a physician. Patients like her. Barly seems to like her. She's a lovely person, Richard. Yet ...

"Yet, what?"

Harriett shrugged her shoulders. "I can't explain it."

———

Dear Mac,

What am I doing?

Playing doctor? Playing nurse?

I've lost my identity in so many ways.

All the while missing you.

Mac, I know now that I love you. All that nonsense of mine, worrying that we were from different worlds. My sweetheart, we are the richer for what we bring to each other.

It's almost Christmas ... if only we were together.

I love you,

Maria

Chapter 25

STELLA WAS IN LOVE.

Actually, she was obsessed with Howie.

Even though he lived in Portsmouth he was from York, and Stella didn't want the gossip mongers to fling around the news of her budding romance. They might jinx her good luck. But confiding her new love to Morgan was different. Morgan didn't know that many people in the village, other than Farnsworth's patients, and from what Stella could tell, Morgan was not a blabbermouth. She kept her private life private. The fact that Morgan suggested they have drinks at her house made it even better—hush-hush, no prying eyes, no one overhearing what she was saying.

For her part, Morgan had news for Stella. It had been almost two weeks since the train episode. Barly had called a few times but didn't say anything more, other than he was swamped with surgeries. But she had not been idle.

Cracking the car window for Jenny, Morgan hurried into the *When Pigs Fly* bakery for a round loaf of multi-grain bread and a jar of their dipping spices. She had a bottle of white wine cooling in the refrigerator at home, plus a bottle of red if Stella preferred.

Morgan had just finished cutting the bread into cubes when Stella arrived brimming over with news of her love affair with Howie. The two friends hugged in greeting. Both had changed after work into turtlenecks and cozy sweats. Seeing Morgan's sock feet Stella kicked off her sneakers and followed her hostess to the living room. Gas flames flickered in the fireplace and Christmas music was playing on the radio.

They settled on the floor in front of the fireplace, backs to the couch, legs stretched out to the side of the low coffee table.

"Red or white," Morgan asked holding up the bottle of Merlot and lifting the Chardonnay from a terra-cotta cooler.

"White, please."

"Okay, Stel, give," Morgan said pouring the wine. "From the flush on your cheeks I have a feeling your big news has to do with Howie. First, tell me how his leg is healing. Did the injury leave him with a limp?"

"Maybe a little," Stella said. "Cheers. Mmmm, this is wonderful and the bread cubes in this olive oil and … what's in the seasoning?"

"I'd have to check the jar. One of the bakery's mixtures. Stop stalling."

"Well, I've told you Howie is a day-trader … all sorts of stocks. You wouldn't believe what I'm learning. He says he doesn't know how he lived without me. Can you believe it?"

"You're still at the office supply shop—"

"Quit today. It feels sooo good."

"Oh, oh. Are you telling me you're moving to Portsmouth?"

"Not right away … that is … well, Howie has inferred that maybe we should live together. Oh, wow. I said it. Morgan, I love this man. Everything about him. He doesn't treat me like I'm an air-head. Nothing like at the office shop where I'm a bookkeeper," she giggled. "Was a bookkeeper, but treated like a salesclerk most of the time."

"Living together. That's a big step, Stel. Do your parents know? Of course, you're a grown woman. You can do what you want—"

"They don't like it one bit but they said they'd keep an open mind. Dad doesn't understand what Howie does … how he can make a living sitting in front of the computer in his slippers. Howie let that slip the first time they met. I think he was trying to impress my mom and dad that he could live at home *and* make scads of money."

Stella paused fortifying herself with a gulp of wine, her eyes sparkling in anticipation of confiding her big news. "Howie does other stuff. He travels to New Hampshire, even Michigan. He said someday maybe he'd take me with him. Imagine, me traveling … with Howard Bond!"

"I take it he travels for business. What kind of business? Something to do with stocks?"

"No, I don't think so," Stella said dipping another cube of bread. "I've asked him but he says not to worry my pretty head about it, and then the next thing I know we're romping around in his bed. Whew, he really knows all about making love," Stella said fanning her face. "I tell you, Morgan, I can't think of anything else but being in his bed. Of course, I've been working weekends for Howie—less than thirty minutes to Portsmouth you know. Oh, my, my, I might as well tell you. But promise to keep it under your hat ... not even Dr. Farnsworth."

"You know I will."

"I'm moving in with Howie this weekend. I can't believe it ... Christmas with him." Stella leaned back against the couch, eyes closed. "Morgan, I do love him and I'm sure he loves me. I've never told anyone, but I picked him in high school as the man I wanted to marry. But he didn't notice me ... until now." Stella opened her eyes, tears of joy spilling down her cheeks.

Morgan wrapped her arms around the love-sick woman, hugging her tight. "I'm so happy for you, Stel."

Leaning away from each other, they laughed, dabbing their eyes with a napkin.

Topping off their wine, the two gazed into the fire. Stella dreaming of Howie, and Morgan wondering if she should divulge what she had been up to the last few weeks.

"Okay, Morgan. Your turn. You said you had news for me."

Sighing, Morgan decided to forge ahead. The fact that Stella wasn't going to be around York come the weekend made it easier. There was less chance of word spreading that the nurse practitioner was soon to be a doctor, that is until she was ready to let it out.

"When my parents died and I left Washington, I was about to take the State Boards to practice ... as a doctor ... a surgeon."

Stella jumped up. "You what? A doctor? A real doctor?"

Alarmed, Morgan looked up. What had she done? Once the words slipped out there was no taking them back. The look of surprise on Stella's face scared her. Stella was shocked. Others would be shocked—question that she could do such a thing. Staring at Stella, Morgan mumbled something about leaving Washington State as an intern ... a resident ... took any job she could get.

Maybe it was a good thing to start with Stella. Seeing the effect on her, Morgan knew she had to think fast, be ready with her story, be ready to expand the biography of the woman from Wenatchee, apple country.

She hadn't been in touch with Agent Donovan since he had established her credentials with the Maine Medical Department administrator, opening the way for her to take the Boards for her license to practice in the state. She'd acted on the opportunity but hadn't told him or Zach. They always wanted to control everything she did.

After divulging more about their secrets, and many hugs, and wishing each other well, promising to keep in touch, Stella was gone.

Suddenly filled with apprehension, Morgan knew she had to call Zach. But not tonight. She needed time to adjust to Stella's reaction.

Agent Donovan had meetings with his counterparts in Boston a couple of days before Christmas and was scheduled to meet with Zach and his witness the next day. She'd tell them both together. Get their full angry blast once instead of twice. Of course, they had cleared the way for her to get her license so it shouldn't be a shock. The problem was her doing it without letting them know. She suspected Donovan had agreed to help her as part of his getting his way, getting her to agree with his bait scheme.

———

Dearest Mac,

I let the cat out of the proverbial bag. I told my friend, my only girlfriend, that I'm going for my license to practice as a doctor in Maine. It's not a bad thing—opens opportunities. Let's say you want to start a fishing charter in Maine. Well, then my sweetheart, we can be together in either Florida or Maine.

Christmas decorations are all over the place up here. I guess it is more traditional than in Florida—pine Christmas trees instead of little lights adorning palm fronds.

Next year will be different. I'm thinking both pine and palm.

All my love,

Yearning to be with you,

Maria

Chapter 26

SNOWFLAKES FLUTTERED FROM THE sky, pristine white crystals piling up on the frozen ground. Morgan clutched a mug of coffee as she gazed out at the wintery scene. The holidays were in full swing and suddenly it was the day before Christmas, the radio playing the season's music non-stop.

There was no Christmas tree in her house. She didn't have the heart to pretend she was in a merry mood. She felt removed, far away, from the place she loved, the man she loved. Yet, for most in York, it was an idyllic day. A day to bake cookies, a day children played outside rolling balls of snow into snowmen, sticking in a carrot nose, coal for button eyes, and their own stocking caps sitting on top of the heads of their sculptures.

I'll be Home for Christmas … the music only heightened her melancholy, thoughts of her mother and Christmases past. Thoughts filled with hope for future holiday celebrations with Mac were eluding her. Checking the mantel clock, there was still time before she had to leave for Boston and her meeting with Agent Donovan and an early dinner with Zach.

Jenny trotted to her side, sat, and smiled. Laughing at her dog's teeth trick without being asked, Morgan grabbed her coat and Jenny's leash. Maybe a walk would help pass the time.

"Come on, Jenny. Let's go out. We both need some fresh air."

Twenty minutes later she stomped the snow from her ankle boots, eagerly entering through the back door of the house with a swoosh of snowflakes. An idea had taken hold of her thoughts, an idea that had her hands shaking. A plan that she was going to put into immediate action before she talked herself out of it.

With a glass of wine, hoping to settle her nerves, Morgan sat down at her computer desk, filled her lungs with air as she picked up the telephone receiver and punched in the number she knew so well.

"Sunrise House, Mrs. Trebly speaking. Can I help you?"

...

"Hello, you've reached Sunrise House. Hello, hello."

"Ah ... sorry. Hello. I'd like to speak to Marianne Grayson. Is she available?"

"Who's calling?"

"I ... I'm her lawyer's secretary. The lawyer who handles her estate. I was asked to make sure this month's check had arrived and to wish her a merry Christmas. Wish her a merry Christmas personally, if that's possible."

"The monthly check did arrive, right on time. Let me transfer you to her room. I know her caretaker is with her, changing the bed linen, so I'm sure she can take your call. It's very kind of you. Please tell the lawyer thank you for the personal remembrance."

...

"Hello, Marianne Grayson's room. You wish to speak with her?"

"Yes ... please."

"Marianne, a phone call for you. Here, dear, take the phone. Hold it to your ear. That's it."

"Hello ... Marianne?" Morgan spoke softly, the words catching in her throat.

"Who's this?"

"I ... I ... merry Christmas, Mother."

The sound of the phone hitting the floor was followed with quick footsteps.

Morgan heard her mother begin to sob ... then the caretaker consoling her.

Heard Marianne callout for someone by the name of Artie.

Then the phone went dead.

———

OVER THREE-THOUSAND MILES away in San Diego a recorder captured a voice addressing Marianne Grayson as mother, wishing her a merry Christmas.

Chapter 27

Boston, Massachusetts

THE WIPERS SWEPT BACK and forth, flicking the fluffy snowflakes from the car's windshield. Morgan felt the back tires slip slightly to the side. Gripping the wheel she turned into the skid, righting the car. Cars sped by her, warriors on the snow-covered road. With no experience driving in snowy conditions, she kept under the speed limit, eyes peeled straight ahead. She came up to a truck spewing sand. Changing lanes, one hand remaining tight on the steering wheel, she held a tissue to her eyes before a tear smeared her makeup.

It had been several hours since Morgan had heard her mother's voice. She was thankful that she was approaching Boston without a mishap, and thankful that Zach had asked her to meet with Donovan at the field office even though it was Christmas Eve, thankful for a reason to get out of the house.

Donovan! He wasn't going to be happy with his star witness.

Zach had promised her an early dinner, a leisure walk through Boston Commons to see the park's trees adorned with thousands of tiny white lights, and to hear joyful Christmas carolers. He also mentioned a stroll by Macy's window displays. These New England traditions were his gifts to her before sending her on her way back to York.

Pulling into the familiar parking garage, joining the bustle of excited holiday shoppers loaded with presents, Morgan felt a tingle of happiness. A small smile played on her lips—she had heard her mother's voice this morning—a wonderful gift.

With a light rap on Zach's door, she stepped into his office. Jumping to his feet, he gave her a brief hug and quickly stepped back, arms dangling by his side. From his reaction, she guessed her shopping spree was a hit. With a few inches of snow over the last few weeks, she figured it was time to invest in a pair of boots, not any boots, small ankle boots with a heel showing from under black, bootleg slacks flaring just enough to see her new footwear. She topped the slacks with a black turtleneck sweater and finished the look with gold hoops.

"Morgan, you look terrific. Any problem parking?"

"No. I managed to find a spot in the garage on Park Street," Morgan said. She tried to laugh but it stuck inside, nerves suddenly surfacing. She knew she had broken their rules but she also knew she'd do it again if she had to.

"Let me take your coat. Agent Donovan will be here shortly. He's anxious to meet with you."

"That I am, Morgan," the agent said strolling in as he held out his hand. "How is everything up north?"

"Fine, thank you. I'm glad we're meeting. There are a couple of things I have to tell you."

Alarm bells immediately went off in Zach's head. He took a seat opposite Morgan, leaned back, hands splayed on the pad of paper he held on his knees, eyes fixed on her.

Donovan pulled up a chair next to Zach. Both men faced her across the worn oak table, a long-time fixture in the old office building. "Okay, tell us—" Donovan started to say.

"I took the State of Maine Boards last week to practice as a doctor." *There, one down one to go.* She looked from one to the other for a reaction. There was none. "What? No comment?"

Donovan was the first to speak. "When do you receive your license and have you told anyone else?"

"Aren't you curious to know if I passed?"

"I'm sure you did, Dr. Grant, which is why I cleared the way, but I didn't know you planned to go through the process so quickly. Now, when do you receive the license and who knows?" Donovan didn't move in his chair. He did not raise his voice. He could have been talking about plans for the weekend.

"I received a call a couple of days ago. As of that call I can precede my name with a D R in Maine. The paperwork will catch up in a few weeks. As to who knows? No one except a close woman friend, Stella Trent." Morgan didn't shrink, spoke in a commanding voice. She may be their witness, but she still had control of a few aspects of her life, emphasis on a few.

Zach hadn't said a word. It was another complication for him to deal with. Morgan thought it was a step forward but she could see that Zach was irritated and hurt that she hadn't told him. She knew he was processing her news, the ramifications on how she was to be protected.

"I don't know how Zach feels, but I applaud what you did. We have to work on your story as to how you were able to pull this off so quickly ... from a nurse to doctor," Donovan said. "But I'm sure, on the positive side, you feel more comfortable ... more comfortable in your new skin."

"Thanks, Alex. I do feel ... more comfortable ... that soon there will be some lies I can put to the side. As for the story, when I told Stella I referenced the death of my parents, dropped everything, and took a job I could easily qualify for—nurse practitioner."

"You said you had a couple of things to tell us," Donovan said. He was now standing next to the case board, arms crossed over his chest, bracing for what she was going to say.

"I'm sorry, but I broke one of your rules this morning. They say confession is good for the soul. I hope you agree."

"What did you do?" Zach asked.

Both agents stared at her, brows drawn together, lips in a thin line.

"I called my mother."

"Morgan, you didn't!" Zach jumped to his feet. Shaking his head in disbelief, he rubbed his bald head, and stomped from one side of the small office to the other. Both men shed their jackets revealing their casual dress—sweaters over trousers over sneakers. It was a holiday.

Donovan, hands on his hips, glared at her. "As you've asked me, how did *you* identify yourself? Did you speak with your mother, and if so what did you say ... *exactly*."

"I used some of your words. I said I was a secretary for the law firm who handles Marianne Grayson's affairs. I never gave a name."

"And?" Donovan prompted. "Did you speak with her?"

"Sort of. My mother said, 'who's this?' I didn't respond directly. I just said merry Christmas. Then it sounded like she dropped the phone and I guess the attendant hung it up."

"Exactly, what did you say to your mother ... precisely?" Donovan asked.

Morgan glared back. "I said merry Christmas, Mother."

They groaned in unison. Donovan looked to the ceiling. Zach slumped in his chair. "We have to relocate you," Zach said.

"Oh, no you don't. I'm not going anywhere else. You have to deal with what I did or I'm out of the program." Morgan glared at Donovan matching his hands-on-hips stance.

"Morgan, you understand you have jeopardized the case to say nothing of putting yourself in danger. If there was a weak link in your vanishing act it was your mother. I'll send somebody out disguised as a ... a technician for a heat and air-conditioning company, or something liked that. Send someone to sweep your mother's room for a bug, plus check where calls come in. Is there a switchboard, a console at a front desk? There must be someone who answers and transfers the calls."

Alex took a breath, looked at Zach then back to Morgan. "Just so you know, Morgan, we still haven't been able to locate DelaCruz but, like it or not, you are now bait. Naturally, I knew of the prospect of your obtaining your license. I think the best course of action is to give us time to check your mother's room for a bug before you add the title of doctor to the problem. If we find one—her room phone or a central unit—then we have to beef up your protection."

Zach hid the creeping apprehension he felt for his witness, the fear of what was ahead of her, and a personal panic for a woman he had begun to care deeply about. Feelings, if he acted upon, were definitely against the rules.

———

ZACH TUCKED MORGAN'S ARM through his. If only he could keep her there until the case was over. But that might be a year or longer. Or, with the bait issue again on the table, only a few weeks. Over dinner he tried to keep the conversation light and didn't mention the issue of her mother. The lights twinkled on the trees as he led her through the Boston Commons, but instead of delight, they sent shivers up his spine. The smiling faces of shoppers looking for that last-minute gifts saddened him.

"What are you doing tomorrow, Morgan, Christmas day?"

"The Farnsworth's invited me for dinner. Harriett too. And, of course, a special bone for Jenny. Harriett and Jenny are best buddies. She insists I drop her off if I'm going to be gone longer than four or five hours. How about you?" They both laughed at her redirection of the conversation.

"I'm flying to Detroit tonight. Spending a few days with my folks. I'll have my cell on me at all times. Don't hesitate for a minute if you notice or feel anything strange." Zach turned her to him. "Do you hear me, Dr. Grant? Don't hesitate a minute. Even if I'm out of the office, I can have an agent by your side in less than an hour or local officers in minutes if you need them."

"I hear you." Morgan gave him a peck on the cheek. "Stop worrying, and, by the way, you'll never know how good that sounds. The Dr. Grant part."

"How do you like the snow?" Zach added, sighing in resignation. "We haven't had a major storm this month, no blizzard, only a few inches."

"Actually I'm doing pretty well, but then I only drive five or ten minutes in any direction. Everything I need is inside what the locals call York Village, except for my trips to Boston. A few days ago Stella—my patient, slash girlfriend, slash confidante—insisted I accompany her shopping at the Kittery outlets. Now, there's a place with some serious shoppers. It was fun. She is totally besotted with Howard Bond. I told you about him—red Corvette, nasty gash on his leg from that pile—"

"Yeah, you told me about him."

"I'm a little concerned about Stella. The first time she wasn't with him, every minute of the day, was when we went shopping at the outlets. He's hired her part time to help with his day-trading accounts, and now she's quit her job and moved in with him. He lives in Portsmouth. Has scads of money—her words. She's very excited. Said she met one of his friends and that Howie was angry about the delay of some sort of shipment. He wouldn't tell her, or maybe she was distracted, what it was … the shipment. I guess he's into all sorts of stuff—again her words."

"Sounds mysterious," Zach said.

"She's smart but I worry her emotions are trumping her brain. I hope she's not getting in over her head. Wouldn't want her to get hurt."

"Morgan, I'm so proud of you, how you've adapted to your new life. I know you're putting on a brave face. It has to be difficult. But please, don't call your mother again … and … I have to ask, you didn't call *that fisherman* did you?"

"Thought about it, but, no, I didn't call *that fisherman*. I told you … *stop worrying*."

Zach folded her in his arms, hoping she took it as a brotherly hug, but feeling anything but brotherly. "Merry Christmas, Morgan, and drive carefully. Looks like we may be in for a white holiday."

———

Merry Christmas sweetheart,

It's just after midnight and the snow is piling up. It took me almost three hours to drive home from Boston—slippery road and several cars in the ditch.

I had a meeting with the agents, told them I called my mother. Oh boy, they were not happy. Broke the rules: no contact with my previous life. Also told them I passed the Maine Boards. I'm now licensed to practice in Maine.

This letter will be short, but long enough to tell you how much I love you. You fill my thoughts, I feel your touch. I feel your kiss. I can only trust that you feel mine.

Good night sweetheart,
Merry Christmas
All my love,
Maria

Chapter 28

York, Maine

CHRISTMAS MORNING, Morgan felt Jenny's cold nose nudging her. Time to get up. Time to go out. Time to play.

Morgan rolled over, stretched and yawned. "Okay, girl. Today is a special day. No moping around for us. Give me your best smile. Teeth!"

Jenny smiled her toothy grin. She had learned not to growl if Morgan was smiling. If she frowned, that was different.

"First you get a big red bow on your collar ... *after* I fix my coffee. Then you and I are going ... wow, Jenny. Look at that. It's a winter wonderland."

Jenny began whining.

"Okay, I'll hurry. Five minutes. That's all I ask."

While Mr. Coffee gurgled in the kitchen, Morgan pulled on knee-high snow boots, not the fancy ones she wore yesterday, her sweatpants, sweater, and parka. With a quick pause in the kitchen for her mug of coffee, she and Jenny ventured into the fairyland of ice crystals.

After a squat on the long-gone flowers, Jenny dashed around rousing the squirrels and, chipmunks, and barking at the birds.

Morgan chose to walk on the road which had been freshly plowed. She figured about eight inches had fallen during the night. No more expected today—sun was bright, the rays sending diamond-like shards of light off everything they touched.

Much planning had gone in to how she was going to spend the day. Barly told her he was visiting family up north in Bangor, so she was on her own. Knowing the day was going to be nostalgic, probably even a real downer, she rented a movie, Humphrey Bogart and Ingrid Bergman in *Casablanca*, and throwing caution to the wind stuffed the refrigerator with traditional fare. A half turkey would go into the oven when she and Jenny returned from their walk—had to have the aroma of turkey circulating through the house. A loaf of frozen bread dough and then an apple pie would be the extent of the festivities. Even though she was having dinner with the Farnsworths late in the day she wasn't going to let her guard down this morning or early afternoon. No feeling sorry for herself.

However, she was only going to infuse the day with just so much Christmas spirit. No holiday music. Several country singers on a couple of Nashville CDs would chase any bad thoughts away that had the nerve to lurk around in her so-called holiday. She had much to be thankful for. She had wished her mother a merry Christmas yesterday, she had passed the Boards, and Donovan and Zach hadn't given her too much grief when she revealed what she had done.

But above all there were warm thoughts of Mac.

Next Christmas would be different. They would hold each other, laugh, cry a little with tears of happiness, and he would make love to her.

Racing with Jenny back to the house, she felt good. More than good. Invigorated. Wonderful! The walk sealed her plan for a Christmas gift to herself. It seemed right. She was going to call Liz. If anyone knew the rules of the game, the game of protecting a witness, it would be Liz and Manny. She would keep the conversation short, revealing nothing, only calling to wish them well. Maybe they would say something about Mac. She certainly could ask how he was.

By two o'clock she was ready to make the call, her present. Comfy in new black yoga pants, and with a glass of wine in hand, she climbed the stairs to her bedroom. Settling into the overstuffed loveseat she had purchased when studying for the Boards, she curled her legs up under her. The music from the radio turned low, she sat gazing out at the trees, their branches painted with snow, a few shadows creeping from their trunks.

With a small sip of wine, she put Liz's business card in her lap and reached for the phone.

"Merry Christmas," Liz answered, a lilt in her voice as always.

"And Merry Christmas to you. Do you recognize my voice?"

"Oh my God. Manny, Manny, it's Maria. Pick up the other phone. Maria, how are you? I love your blonde hair. Where are you?"

"I can't talk long … shouldn't be talking at all, and please don't call me, but ever since you gave me your card I've wanted to call. Donovan … you met him I think, maybe not, doesn't matter, he'd be furious. Are you two married?"

"Not, yet," Manny piped up. "She's keeping me waiting."

"Next month … a few weeks. Maria, I don't know what I'm saying. Oh yeah, that was a handsome guy you were with … when we saw you … Manny thought I was crazy … but I knew your laugh. So who was the guy?"

"A friend. You know I can't say much."

"Well, the way he was looking at you I'd say he was more than a friend. I'm happy for you … your new life."

"It's hard, Liz. Very hard. Manny, have you and Liz been fishing?"

"Oh, yes. In fact Mac has invited us over after the wedding—"

"At the Sandbar. You remember that romantic place, Maria?" Liz interjected.

"Yes. I know your wedding will be lovely."

"Anyway, Mac's giving us a day out in the Gulf, with just him, his pops, and Flo."

"Flo?"

"Yeah. Mac was devastated when he was told you were … oh God, Maria, I'm sorry. Of course, Manny and I were skeptical … you know … I can't say it. Anyway, Mac began to believe what the police told him, and Danny, you remember his pops, of course, you do. Anyway, Danny has been telling him that he should move on, get married. That he, too, had lost the love of his life but married another woman who gave him a son. Gave him Mac. Danny told me all that. Tragic. Do you think that you and that guy, the one in your new life, that you'll move on with him?"

…

"Maria, are you there?"

"Ah … yes. I have to go. Merry Christmas."

Tears welled up in Morgan's eyes. The tears turned to sobs. She'd lost him. She'd lost Mac.

Falling onto the bed, drawing the pillow to her body, knowing she would never feel his arms around her again, she sobbed until the pillow was wet, until her throat was sore. Her heart was broken. Mac had moved on.

Dragging herself from the bed, she made another call. She told Richard that she was sorry but she wouldn't be joining them for dinner. She was sick.

Barly called but she didn't pick up.

Zach, Stella, and Harriett called. She answered none of them.

All people in her new life. A life she didn't want. A life that was thrust upon her.

Slowly putting one foot in front of the other she went to the kitchen. The turkey sitting on the platter ready to be sliced and the apple pie were wrapped in foil returning them to the refrigerator. The bread baked to a golden brown went into a bag and returned to the freezer.

Pouring another glass of wine, she shuffled to the living room and turned on the television. Sitting in the shadows that faded to night, she stared at the black and white movie on the screen—*It's a Wonderful Life.*

———

HOURS PASSED. MORGAN thrashed about under the covers, finally flinging them to the floor as she sat up.

She looked at the clock on the bedside table.

12:01 a.m.

Christmas was over!

With a deep breath she straightened her spine, swung her legs over the edge and stood tall. Jenny lifted her head from her doggie bed, saw her mistress wasn't leaving the room, and laid her head back down.

With three deliberate steps, Morgan walked to the lamp table beside the loveseat, a piece of furniture that would be replaced in the morning. Reaching for her cell, she tapped the number stored in the directory.

"Donovan here. Morgan, is something wrong?"

"I want you to get the bastard. I want you to get the bastard who stole my life. I want you to get the bastard who is in the business of destroying other people's lives. Yes, I'll be the bait. Write me into your script."

Chapter 29

THE SUN SPARKLED IN the frigid nineteen degree air as the ski plane set down softly on the frozen water of Moosehead Lake and taxied to the dock. The bush pilot kept the plane idling as Barly stepped on a ski and then onto the dock. He turned raising his hands, catching Morgan in his arms, setting her on her feet beside him.

His passengers safely on the dock, the bush pilot tossed two small bags to Barly. "I delivered your grocery and wine orders yesterday and turned up heat enough to take off the chill. Have a nice New Year's Eve and of course a Happy New Year," the pilot called out a grin spreading over his face.

"Thanks, Tim. I think we're good for a couple of days. I'll call you, probably the third, early afternoon. Are there still some five-gallon cans of gas for the snowmobiles?"

"Yup, checked it myself just as you asked. Okay, doc, I'll be off but watch the weather. There's a report of a front moving in from the Atlantic. Wouldn't want you two to get marooned," he said chuckling as he pulled the door shut.

Morgan watched the little plane gain speed until it was airborne. "I feel like I'm in a painting. Do you always travel this way?"

"It's over a four-hour drive up here from York. So in answer to your questions, yes, and no. I don't own a plane. With my schedule, and being on call at the hospital, it's cheaper to fly up. I do have a pilot's license, but the cost to keep a plane sitting in a hangar doesn't make sense. Besides, on the lake there's the issue of pontoons in summer and skis when the lake freezes over."

He hoisted his duffle bag over his shoulder and took the handle of her case from her hand. "Come on, I'll start a fire, open some vino, and then show you around."

Morgan lagged behind. She was moving on. She was determined to move on. Between the tears, the irrational feelings of betrayal that he had forgotten her so quickly, or the more rational feeling that she had lost him. Or, coming to grips with the thought that maybe she had misread Mac's attention. Whatever it was, she had accepted Barly's invitation—a retreat from reality over the New Year's holiday.

Turning in a circle several times, she marveled at the beauty, the isolation, the serene quiet of Moosehead Lake. Ahead, was an A-frame style house on a slight rise. A wrap-around deck with soaring windows framed the west-facing side of the structure, a structure Barly had described as a cottage. It certainly wasn't like any cottage she had ever seen before. This was another dimension of Dr. Joe Bartholomew. Smiling, she quickly caught up with him.

Entering the cottage, Barly helped her out of the parka he had provided for the flight. "There are two bedrooms at the top of the stairs, in the loft, and a private bathroom. Take your pick. Settle in while I start that fire."

Giving him a peck on the cheek, she grabbed her overnight bag. "Thanks, I won't be long."

The so-called bedroom took up the front of the loft. Peeking in the room down a short hall she found another bedroom, much smaller. It was cozy but not as spectacular as the one in front overlooking the living room below, and providing a magnificent view of the lake through the soaring living room windows. Snow traced the scene in sparkling white. *A Currier and Ives painting,* she thought.

Selecting the front bedroom was an easy choice. The bed was covered with a quilt appliquéd with bursts of colorful flowers, and lined at the head with pillows of various sizes in colors to match the flowers in the quilt. A yellow butterfly sun catcher hung in the window to the side of the bed. Placing the few pieces of clothing she packed into the chest of drawers by a bookcase, she pulled on a white cable-knit sweater over her black turtleneck shirt. At the foot of the bed was a pair of slipper socks, bottoms made of soft leather. Delighted with the idea of socks, she pulled them on under her caramel colored wool slacks.

Hearing the crackle of the fire from the stone fireplace below, she stepped down the staircase to join her host. At each step in the curved staircase a different painting was revealed. The art depicting the life and struggles of Native Americans—harvesting corn, hunting deer and moose, ritual dances to the Gods. All were painted in vivid colors of blue, gold, green and red, predominately of red. The contrast of the art against the rough cedar walls was breathtaking.

"Everything okay in the bedroom?" Barly asked handing her a goblet of red wine.

"I'm blown away. Tell me about your art collection. It seems very personal."

Barly's gray eyes were warm gazing into her beautiful face framed in strands of gold. "You're the first to notice. My mother is a Native American, Algonquin tribe. The tribe spilled into the States from Canada. Many learned the ways of the white man. Over time, more and more were educated in American schools, learned trades which turned into careers, businesses. My father met mom in an art gallery where she was invited to display her paintings."

"You must have some of her work. Please, show me—"

"They're all hers." Barly laughed. "She's very prolific. I've told her if she keeps it up, I'll have to build a wing on the house. These are the only ones I was able to buy before someone else bought them up."

The firelight played on the paintings as Barly told her about each one—the choice of colors, the composition, the meaning his mother was trying to portray. Twice he topped off their wine glasses.

"The paintings are wonderful, this house is wonderful, the lake, the snow, your choice of CDs—Beethoven's Moonlight Sonata. It's as if we're in another world—safe ... no intruders."

"Intruders?"

"Visitors. You mentioned a snowmobile to Tim. Is there a garage I didn't see?"

"Not exactly. I call it a wood shed. A big wood shed. Right now, there's a four-wheel drive Range Rover, two snowmobiles, a snow blower, and about fifteen-cords of wood—give or take. And, a few pairs of cross-country skis." He tapped her glass with his. "We'll start the year off right tomorrow with a trek through the pines on the boards."

"I was afraid you were holding that scheme in your mind. I told you I've never been on skis."

"A girl from Washington State with all those mountains? That's hard to believe, and something I plan to remedy in the morning."

Morgan turned away, took a few steps to look out the windows. *Washington. Watch yourself, Morgan. Don't spoil this retreat.* "Jenny would love it here. I can just see her scampering through the snow. What's that heavenly smell? Pot roast?"

"My dear, I'll have you know that is the specialty of the Mountain Inn in Greenville on the southern tip of the lake, a few miles from here— beef bourguignon—a hearty supper to bolster the body for a day of activity tomorrow."

"Let me help. Just where are we going to enjoy this feast? The big harvest table seems much too austere and besides the fire is—"

"My thoughts exactly. The coffee table by the fireplace will do. If you'll pick up the knives and forks, second drawer on your right, and the plates, cupboard above, I'll serve up our dinner. Mmmm, just smell that roast. And I see they included their famous mashed potatoes with garlic, green beans, and a loaf of bread. I'll zap the bread in the microwave. You'll find a tub of butter in the fridge."

"And just how did this magnificent food magically appear in your house?"

"A long-standing arrangement with the owners of the inn. In return, the owners have the use of my snowmobiles, car, anything they need. When I was overseeing the building of this place I stayed in Greenville … at their inn."

Sitting on cushions on opposite sides of the coffee table, the fire blazing, they both stripped off their sweaters chuckling at each other's black turtleneck shirts.

"You enjoy your life don't you, Barly. Your toys, this cottage—"

"Toys?"

"A plane at your beck and call, lovely meals at beautiful places overlooking the Atlantic, a snowmobile, skis, this hideaway."

"Well, I do have dreams. Coffee?"

"Yes, please. I'll clear the table. What kind of dreams?" Morgan asked stacking the dishes in the dishwasher as the coffeemaker gurgled to life.

"You can't tell anyone. My dreams are secret. Milk? Sugar?"

"Half and half if you have it."

"Coming right up." Barly poked the fire adding two more logs then pushed the coffee table to the side so they could lean back against the couch.

Morgan waited. She could tell he was thinking it over—should he divulge his dreams to her or not?

"Have you ever thought about doing something important with your life?" he asked staring at a burst of flames.

Waiting for him to define important, she added a splash of cream to her coffee and held the small carton up to him. He shook his head.

"When I'm operating, holding someone's heart in my hands, their life, I've often wondered about those who die young—children, babies, because they don't have access to the medical care such as where you and I work every day."

"You mean poor people in third-world countries?"

"Could be, but I'd rather help people in our country. So many wonderful human beings who need a hand up, but held back because of problems with their health, their bodies consuming their attention—no way to fix their condition. Just think, we could travel our great nation, help so many, most of which would be pro-bono, all because we were so lucky to have the opportunity, the means, and fortitude to be trained in the medical profession."

She noticed as he was speaking of his dreams, that his choice of words changed from I to we. Surely he wasn't including her in his dream. Or was he? His excitement was catching.

"It's not only the young, the poor, who could use your help, there's our military. Men and women who are suffering, gave up so much for us," Morgan said.

Barly turned to her, leaning his elbow on the seat of the couch. "You're so right. And the wonderful part of this is that we could do it forever. Retirement is a word that should be banned, except in planning financially. People should plan what they want to do with their lives after their nine-to-five jobs. Fulfillment in those later years doesn't just happen you know. I bet you've seen patients who have this and that ailment stemming from boredom. Such a waste. I don't want that. Don't get me wrong, I'll still have time to enjoy my toys," he said smiling.

Morgan gazed into the fire. *It would be so nice to be in control of your life. Barly can do whatever he wants; go wherever his dreams take him. Maybe someday I can too. It would be so nice to be part of a dream like his, work together with someone you care about ... loved.* She sighed.

"I'm sorry. I didn't mean to go on." He squared his back against the couch.

"Thank you for sharing your secret with me. I believe, Dr. Bartholomew, that you will make your dreams a reality some day."

"Hey, look at the clock. It's almost midnight and I have a bottle of champagne in the fridge. Are you up for bringing in the New Year with a glass, or do you want to turn in?"

"Well, you have laid out a big day tomorrow, but I can't imagine a more perfect setting to welcome a new year. Champagne, please."

"If you'll rescue the flutes from the freezer, I'll pop the cork and we'll get this celebration underway. Let's put our sweaters on ... nothing like champagne out on the deck under the stars."

"I have the flutes."

"Okay, here, slip on this parka and let's go."

A fresh coating of snow scrunched under their slipper socks as they walked to the front of the deck. Leaning against the railing, Barly put his fingers to his lips, then pointed to a moose taking a stroll to the lake. "Chilly out here. Are you warm enough?" he whispered.

"Toasty."

"Happy New Year, Morgan."

"Happy New Year, Barly."

Clinking their glasses, Barly kissed her lips gently. Pulling away he looked into her eyes fixated on his. He took her glass placing it to the side on the snow-covered picnic table. He gathered her into his arms unable to resist the urge to hold her, kiss her, taste her, inhale her perfume. Breathing hard, he pulled back again, running his fingers through her blonde waves.

"Morgan, I didn't plan for this to happen when I invited you up here. But I was fooling myself if I didn't dream of it."

"Another dream?"

"Let's go in by the fire, have another glass of champagne ...

Morgan felt a tug on her heart. He wasn't the only one kidding himself. Her heart was racing, her body hot, longing to be held. No other thought had room in her mind, only of Barly, a man wanting her … she wanting him. The fire blazed hot in front of them, around them, through them.

"Morgan, I've wanted you like this since I first laid eyes on you." His mouth dropped to hers, his lips tasted the salt of sweat on her neck. She arched against him as he revealed her beautiful body one piece of clothing after another … slowly … slowly to her slacks, to her silky panties edged in lace. "Tell me now if you want to stop us … us … you and me."

"Us." Her eyes holding his, her body pressed against him glistening in the flickering flames.

Chapter 30

THE SUN STREAMED IN through the window warming Morgan's face, the warm caress urging her eyes to open to a new day, a new year. Curled up in Barly's arms the realization of what she had done sent nerves pinging throughout her system.

Oh my God. Think. Think.

Her breathing quickened, lungs filling then expelling air her only movement. Barly had guided her to his bed. Now, in the bright morning sun, she saw a heavy gray-down quilt covering their naked bodies.

Remaining still her eyes roamed about the room, what she could see of it lying on her side. A heavy golden-toned oak dresser stood against the wall by the window. A geometrically patterned rug in hues of black, gray, red, and various shades of butterscotch, more than likely designed by his mother, covered her side of the floor.

She slipped out from under the quilt, stood a minute looking at her lover. Lover? Suddenly Barly's tousled hair became Mac's, his eyes piercing her heart.

Shaking her head she fled the room on tiptoe. Picking up her clothes scattered in front of the fireplace, she tiptoed up the stairs to dress.

Coffee, that's what I need. A new year. Has to be better than the old. You have some serious thinking to do, missy.

Her cell rang. Where is it? There … her shoulder bag under her slacks. Grabbing for it she sat on the bed, the bed she should have slept in last night.

"Harriett?"

"Thank God you're there," Harriett said. "I've been trying to reach you. Are you all right?"

"Happy new year, Harriett. Yes, I'm fine. What's up?"

"Someone broke into your house yesterday. Not exactly broke in. I came over to pick up some more dog food. Jenny certainly does like to eat. Probably invigorated with the cold air—"

"Harriett, the door. Maybe it wasn't latched when I left. What makes you think someone was in the house?"

"Jenny. She acted very strange. Ran all over, nose to the floor, barking crazy like."

"Was anything broken?"

"Not that I can see. Of course, I can't tell if anything was taken … I don't know what's yours or what the Thaxters left in the house."

"Did you call the police?"

"No. That's why I've been trying to reach you. Didn't know if you, like you said, didn't close the door tight … especially because I don't see anything disturbed."

"I'm coming home but it may be late. I'm not sure how—"

"Morgan? Hey, you up there?"

Morgan looked over the loft railing. Barly was standing barefoot in jeans and his signature black turtleneck, his hair tousled. It could have been Mac standing there except for the hair—salt and pepper, not Mac's inky black.

"Harriett, I have to go. Don't do anything … about the door. I'll let you know later when I'll be over to pick up Jenny."

Closing her cell, Morgan looked down at Barly. "I have to go home."

"I know. The front that Tim warned us about has organized into what we call a nor'easter. I'm afraid we could get stranded. With a bad storm coming I'm sure they'll be calling me into the hospital. Farnsworth will probably be looking for you as well. Come on down. The coffee's ready. We can at least salvage something of our day," he said smiling up at her.

Morgan turned away. Someone had been in her house. Her stomach twisted. Fear rose through her body, her skin turning cold.

Stuffing the few things she had put in the dresser into her suitcase, she went into the bathroom catching sight of the person in the mirror. She didn't recognize her. Who was she?

Her fingers gripped the edge of the white porcelain sink. The blonde, brown-eyed woman in the mirror looked back at her. "He's found you," the blonde whispered. "Agent Donovan was right. Like it or not someone snapped at the bait."

Barly met her at the bottom of the stairs with a mug of coffee, steam curling up from the coffee laced with cream. No sugar.

"Thanks," she said, her fingers wrapping around the pottery, its warmth soothing.

"What's the matter?" He took the mug from her fingers setting it on the table and wrapped her in his arms. "Last night was wonderful, Morgan. You—"

"It was a mistake, Barly. A magical night that never should have happened." Squirming from his arms, she picked up the coffee and walked to the front window wall. "When can we expect Tim? I have to get back."

"Oh, no you don't. You're not retreating behind that wall of yours," he said frustrated. His voice raised. "Not after I finally pierced the walls, the walls you hide behind. Last night was not magic, Morgan. It was real. It happened. And now … now you've slipped away from me. Well, I want you back. What was that phone call about?"

"It was Harriett. She thinks someone might have broken into my house. She—"

"Well, no wonder you're concerned. I would be too. I already called Tim. He should be here in an hour to pick us up. I'll come home with you to check that your house is okay. Did Harriett say there was any damage?"

"No."

"That's good," he said standing beside her, but Morgan continued to stare out the window, her wall between them.

"No, means, no. I don't want you to come with me to check my house."

"Morgan, what the hell is going on?" he yelled. He couldn't reach her. He paced to the fireplace, turned but only saw the back of the woman he wanted. God help him, he was in love with her. He was in love with the woman he held in his arms last night. Not this one.

"Nothing is going on," she yelled back. "Nothing! I said last night was a mistake!" *I can't do this anymore*, she screamed in her head. *Donovan has to wrap up this case quickly or I'm out. I put Mac in danger and now Barly. DelaCruz kills to get what he wants. Kills to rid of himself of anyone standing in his way. Out. Out. I want out.*

"Why are you yelling?" he shouted.

"Ask yourself why you're yelling," she shouted back.

"I'm yelling because I care about you. And, I think you're yelling because you care about me and for some reason you don't want to. What are you hiding, Ms. Grant? Tell me that. What's the secret so big you can't tell me? Can't let me help you? What is it, Ms. Grant?"

Chapter 31

York, Maine

THE DRONE OF THE engine filled the cabin of the small ski plane as it approached York. Tim kept her at full throttle with one eye on the thickening clouds and the other on the short, unmanned, landing strip. The bush pilot was anxious to drop off his two silent passengers. Anxious to return his precious plane to her hangar in Greenville before the gale-force winds of the looming nor'easter tossed him around like the snowflakes that had begun to fall.

Barly stared at Morgan's back. She sat strapped into her seat, back straight, eyes fixed on the snowy sky out the small window. The ride was rough, cross currents from the approaching storm buffeting the small craft.

After a bumpy landing on the snow, Morgan thanked Tim for the safe trip back to York. And then, with a firm grip on her bag, she thanked Barly for showing her Moosehead Lake and left him standing on the snow-covered cement with snowflakes licking at his face, the wind flapping his trousers against his legs.

Tim took off heading due north as she drove off to Scituate Road without a hint to Barly of the roiling going on in her stomach, and Harriett's warning of a break-in still echoing in her ears.

Alone in her car, pummeled by the increasing wind gusts, her eyes remained glued to the road mindful of the distance she was putting between herself and Barly. Barly left standing alone without an explanation for her actions other than a possible intruder, nothing about the real reason why she wanted to get away, wanted to leave him.

Fishing around in her shoulder bag, she pulled out her cell and called Zach. With the forecast of the impending storm he had left his parent's home in Detroit and was driving from Boston's Logan Airport to his condo when he answered her call. He instructed her to stay in her house after she picked up Jenny from Harriett's. He would be there in an hour. He also told her not to use the house phone, only answer calls when the display showed the caller was someone she knew, and even then not to say too much. She should keep mum, especially on anything about where, when, or what she was doing. And, she must make all of her outgoing calls on her cell.

"Morgan, don't touch anything. Open the front door with gloves on. I'll dust the knob and frame for fingerprints. Oh, and keep Jenny by your side when you look around the house. I'm sure whoever was there has gone, but you never know."

Morgan picked up Jenny, mumbling thanks and a happy new year to Harriett and continued on home.

She did as she was told. With a gloved hand she unlocked the front door and stepped in. Seeing no one, feeling she was alone, she shut the door behind her. "Come on, Jenny, let's go upstairs. We have to arm ourselves before we check the house."

Jenny cocked her head, trotting close to her mistress as she mounted the stairs, switching on the lights as she went. The cloud cover had plunged the little house into a shadowy gray.

Placing her small case on the bed, Morgan opened the drawer of the nightstand and retrieved her revolver. The same revolver she kept in the nightstand on Anna Maria Island in Florida.

Sitting on the edge of the bed she looked at her dog. Jenny sat close, her muzzle nudging Morgan's knee. "Yes, pretty girl, I'm happy to be home, too. It's just you and me. Harriett said you ran around crazy-like. I'm not sure what you would have done if an intruder popped out of a closet. Jenny, it's not playtime. You have to learn to turn that smile to a deranged attack dog when you show your *teeth*." Morgan emphasized the word teeth to which Jenny happily grinned with a low guttural growl—her mistress was not smiling. However, the dog's fluffy tail was brushing the floor, a dead giveaway that she was ready to play not attack.

"Okay, ferocious one, let's check the house." Elbow bent, Morgan pointed the gun at the ceiling with her right hand, a glove on her left for doorknobs, as she and Jenny checked every room, every closet, under every bed, and behind the couch. Then she carefully stepped down the steep stairs leading from the trapdoor to the cellar. At every turn, Morgan kept her eyes peeled for anything missing or out of place.

Satisfied they were alone she fed Jenny, replenished her bowl with fresh water, and poured herself a glass of wine. After letting Jenny out to do her business, Morgan returned to her bedroom with her companion. She felt safer with a flight of stairs between her and the front door. She sank into the rocking chair that Mrs. Thaxter had left. A favorite chair left behind, along with the rest of her furniture, fully intending to return to her home one day no matter what her son said.

Morgan set the revolver on the nightstand just as her cell rang.

"Morgan, is everything okay?" Zach asked.

"Yes. Jenny and I just finished our patrol. No bad guy. What's that sound? I can barely hear you?"

"Snowplows. I can't get through. No cars allowed on I-95. I'm not going to be able to get to you until tomorrow morning … or whenever they open the highway. Looks like a bad one. Anything disturbed in the house?"

"No. Maybe, as I said, I didn't shut the door tight."

"Morgan, you would have checked the door when you left, probably more than once. I called Donovan. He's sending up an agent to perform a sweep of the house for bugs but the forensics guy is stuck in Boston as I am. We'll both be with you tomorrow, as soon as possible. Morgan, Donovan and I think DelaCruz traced your call to your mother."

"So then, I ask you, Zach, how quick can you get him … DelaCruz? I want out of the program. I have to get my life back."

———

Dear Mac,
Scratch that. He's gone. Remember?
Dear Diary,
I'm scared.
I know he's found me.
My life, old and new, maybe coming to an end.
I also know that Jenny and I will fight.
I'll shoot anyone who tries to kill us.

I just pray that I shoot first.
Morgan

Chapter 32

AT 4:33 A.M. MORGAN'S cell rang. It was Zach.

"Sorry, I didn't want to scare you by ringing the doorbell. We're here, Kenny and I, Donovan's forensic guy. Outside."

Still in her black yoga pants, she ran down the stairs to greet them.

Stomping the snow off their boots, the two agents entered the house along with a blast of freezing cold air. Zach hugged Morgan as he passed her holding the door open. Kneeling on the floor he scratched behind Jenny's ears, his eyes darting around the living room.

The men threw their boots in the box by the front door, parkas on the couch, leaving them dressed in jeans, sweaters, and socks. Jenny checked out the stranger, sniffing his pant legs as Zach made the introductions. He then led the way to the kitchen, his eyes continuing to scrutinize the area as he walked. Morgan put Mr. Coffee to work and soon the aroma mixed with the gurgling of a twelve-cupper pot of coffee. Retrieving the loaf of bread she baked on Christmas day, she popped it in the microwave on defrost.

Zach watched Morgan setting out the mugs, cream and sugar, and napkins. She looked in control, but the slight tremor of her hand gave her away.

While the coffee brewed, Kenny checked her phones—kitchen, bedroom, and computer room. He returned to the pre-dawn coffee klatch empty handed and with a stern face.

"The phones are all bugged. I left them in place. Donovan said he'd set up a video conference via Skype as soon as I let him know what I found. But, I sure would like a cup of that coffee first, and is that fresh baked bread I smell?" Kenny said plugging in his laptop with a camera nub attached to the top edge of the screen.

Morgan laughed, a little chuckle. *Maybe she's starting to relax,* Zach thought.

"Bread is from Christmas. Frozen." After putting out plates, knives, butter, and jam, Morgan joined the men at the table. Zach had already filled the three mugs.

Deliberately ignoring why they were meeting at such an hour, the three chit-chatted about their escapades over the holidays. Morgan outdid them all with a ride on a ski plane into the wilds of Maine. She stopped there.

Fortified with the strong coffee, Kenny called Donovan. At 5:15 a.m. the video conference convened—Donovan in Washington D.C., Zach, Kenny, and Morgan rearranging their chairs so they could all watch as they sipped their coffee, and retrieved slices of bread from the toaster.

"Happy New Year, Morgan. How are you holding up?" Donovan asked his voice strong but filled with compassion, looking at her through the monitor.

"I'm okay. As for the new year? Happy will be when this is over."

"I understand. First, I want you to know that Kenny swept your fisherman's boat and his house. I asked Kenny not to tell you until he and Zach were with you."

Morgan glanced at Kenny, then Zach, then back to Donovan. "And?"

"Both were bugged—boat and house," Kenny said topping off the three mugs. "Macintyre doesn't know I was there or what I discovered. Again, I left the devices as I found them."

Morgan put on another pot. *So, now Mac is in the middle of this for sure. My God, what am I going to do? He's in danger.* Pushing the button on Mr. Coffee, she retrieved the turkey from the freezer, setting it in the microwave on defrost.

"Hey, I want a slice of that hot bread," Donovan teased.

"All you need is a magic snowmobile, boss. Come on up," Kenny chuckled.

Zach and Morgan managed a smile, but this meeting was no laughing matter.

Donovan's face was replaced with the case board on the screen of Kenny's laptop. He added the bugs just found in Morgan's house.

Case: Delacruz Cartel		
Target: Junior DelaCruz, missing Crime: Murder, Gun Running, Drugs Last seen!: Anna Maria Island, FL, 4 months ago	Believed he killed: √Perez Studs Wally	Known Bugs Mother-2 Mac-2 Morgan-3
—	—	...

"Obviously, whoever placed the bugs has us at a disadvantage. He knows where you are and those you care about, but we don't know who installed them, who's listening, or where they are. But, I believe the bugs were placed by one of Junior's men."

"I told you to write me into the script. So write. Bugs on Mac's boat, my mother's room, and now my house." Morgan leaned forward, her eyes piercing Donovan's through the screen.

"A sting!" Donovan said. "We have to set up an operation where we draw DelaCruz out, draw him to you. That's the script."

"Bait. Set me out there. Lure him in?" Morgan asked.

Zach laid his hand over hers letting her know he was, and would be, with her.

Donovan looked back at her. "That's right. Are you sure you're ready to play this part?"

"Positive. How do we do it?"

"Not sure, yet. I'm putting together a plan with Zach and a SWAT force. Our one advantage is that we know about the bugs. We know that they can hear your calls, know that they are listening. We'll use that when we're ready. Soon. All DelaCruz wants is to eliminate your testimony. BUT, he has to be careful he's not charged with another murder, or worse, caught in our net losing his freedom for life."

Chapter 33

ZACH AND KENNY RETURNED to Boston to meet with Donovan, who had flown up from D.C. Morgan was antsy, pacing, wondering where the intruder had stepped. She was barely hanging on to her nerves, about ready to cry hysterically—life was closing in on her.

She had to get out of the house, so she called her friend. A friend she trusted.

Stella jumped at the invitation. She too needed a friend. Her new love was tied up in his work and she was feeling lonely. Maybe they could help each other get out of the doldrums.

It was mid-afternoon when Morgan entered the dimly lit bar in Portsmouth. A scraggly Christmas tree remained on the edge of the bar where it curved, leaving only room for the bartender to squeeze through to deliver drinks. Bing Crosby was crooning *White Christmas*. Morgan wondered why the bartender hadn't switched CDs.

Seeing Stella in a booth at the back, she walked by the other lonely hearts sitting at the bar, staring into their drinks, or trying to crack a joke to the person sitting on the barstool next to them.

Stella leaned into the wall of the bench, feet up, ruby lips in a half smile as Morgan sauntered up. *Stel looks exactly how I feel. No ho-ho-ho for us,* she thought.

Stella managed to untangle her feet long enough to receive Morgan's hug then slumped back on the bench, ankles crossed, staring at her friend.

"You look awful," Stella said.

"I was thinking the same thing about you."

Smiling, the bartender asked for Morgan's order.

"Christmas is over. There must be something else in your collection besides Christmas. Maybe *Winter Wonderland* or *April in Paris*," Morgan said.

"Okay, I'll change the order of the CDs. You two look like you could use something a little cheerier. Frosty the Snowman?" he joked chuckling as he strolled behind the bar to mix Morgan's martini with one, no, two olives. Pushing the button to advance the CD player he laughed when the Chipmunks began belting out their holiday medley.

Neither woman seemed capable of conversation, content to just be with a friend. Friends sometimes do that for each other—remain silent, silent support.

Morgan nodded to the bartender, picked up the stemmed glass with the stuffed olives looking up at her, and tapped Stella's bottle of beer. "Happy New Year. So where's Howie?"

"My guy says he's busy. Had to scurry up to Whitefield of all places."

"Where's that? Never heard of it," Morgan said closing her eyes with a sip of her cold drink.

"New Hampshire, up north. Left yesterday. Said he'd be back late today. Can you beat that? It's still the holidays, well, a few days after, but—"

"At least you know who you are," Morgan said staring into the eyes of the olives.

"That's a funny thing to say. You work in a nice doctor's office, talk to people every day. Not a lonely little condo. Howie's place is really small, cramped. Funny I didn't notice when I first stayed overnight with him."

"I thought he was doing well with his trading?" Morgan replied. *Stella's face is so drawn, depressed.*

"A few bad trades he said. I thought we were moving into some swanky condo, bigger, on the ocean. That's what he told me anyway. But, he says everything will change soon. He'll have money—he kisses me and I melt in his arms. He makes love to me and I swear I'd do anything for him."

"There's more to life than where you live, Stel. Someday... maybe I'll go back to being who I was before."

"Yeah? And who were you before?"

"It doesn't matter."

"Sure it matters, even if it's only a dream."

"My dream … a doctor who saves lives, cuts out bad stuff from their bodies, stitches them back together."

"Pretty grim dream, Morgan. You sound more depressed than I am."

"That's just it, Stel. It's not grim. You can't imagine how thrilling it is to bring a patient back from the brink—"

"So, you said you passed the test to practice … your dream came true. Everything is going your way, Morgan. You'll be hanging out your shingle soon, announcing you are now a doctor."

"I can't do anything on my own."

"Why not? Doctors can do anything they want."

Morgan leaned forward. "I'm a government witness … in hiding," she whispered, popping out a colored lens. One brown eye and one violet eye looked back at Stella.

Stella pulled away, shrank into the back of the booth. "Who are you?"

"Stel, I'm Morgan, your friend."

Chapter 34

NIGHTFALL LENGTHENED THE shadows throughout the cramped condo—stacks of computer printouts alongside gun catalogs piled by the computer desk. Three monitors to display streaming quotes from markets around the world were lined up in back of a keyboard. Colorful, heavy plastic crates lined the living room walls, filled with stock reports, corporate rating sheets, and books promising the latest on how to make a killing in the market.

Stella switched on a table lamp, the aroma of a pot roast in the oven signaled it was time to set the table. Howie had called saying she could expect him in an hour and then hung up. With a couple of candles, a bottle of wine, and a sexy navy blue dress showing off her light olive skin and ample cleavage, Stella hoped her efforts would brighten Howie's disposition. She was in no mood for another fight.

Still stunned by Morgan's news, feeling a bit betrayed by her friend for not telling her sooner, she fantasized about her own situation. Her friend was leading an exciting life, but she seemed to be stuck in a relationship with Jekyll and Hyde—one minute amorous, the next ignoring her.

Maybe tonight Howie would think she was exciting. Look at her as he used to, a bright, interesting woman, especially now that she had a story to tell.

Hearing him remove his boots at the door, she hurried to greet him, glancing around at the room—candlelight, soft music—surely he would be happy to see her.

Howie brushed by Stella throwing his coat on the back of the couch. He looked around at the living-dining room, then at her. "Get dinner out. I'm starved," he ordered as he passed the pretty table, walking directly into the kitchen. He poured three fingers of whiskey in a glass, returned to the dining alcove and slumped in his chair at the end of the table.

Stella served the pot roast and poured wine into her glass. Dinner was silent, punctuated only by the occasional sound of a knife drawing across a plate, a fork stabbing a piece of meat. She waited. Ate her dinner, drank her wine, knowing it was better not to irritate him. Give him time to unwind.

"You seem out of sorts, Howie. What happened in Whitefield?"

"No show." Finishing his drink, he leaned away from the table. "Come here, I need to relax, and, baby, you know how to relieve your Howie's tension." A smile in anticipation that her Howie was back, she rose, slipped into his outstretched arm. Rising, he took her hand, pulled her along to the bedroom. Her smile turned to a frown, his finger's digging into her wrist.

"Okay, but no rough stuff. I don't like it."

"Okay, okay, let's take a shower. You like that. Maybe a smoke."

"Yeah, a shower is good. No weed."

The steamy water felt wonderful on her skin, warming her, but the shower was brief. Howie turned off the water, his pasty-white skin from hours in front of the computer, glistening in the steamy enclosure. He kissed her hard. "Who do you love?"

"Howie, I love you. Honest, I do."

"That's right, baby, you love your Howie," he said flopping on the bed, pulling her to him. He was quickly satisfied leaving Stella panting for more, but Howie had no more to give.

She lay next to him, eyes wide. "Are you going to ask what I did while you were away?"

"Ummm, what did you do, baby?" he said pulling her on top of him.

Maybe there is more if I tease him a little, she thought, her fingers slowly playing with the hair on his chest. "I had drinks with Morgan. You'll never guess what she said."

"Ahhh, I like that. Kiss your Howie, baby."

Stella leaned up, ran her tongue over his lips, then snuggled under his chin. *I can play his game … leave him wanting more.* "She's a witness of some sort … for the government. She's in hiding. Disguised—"

Howie pushed Stella off him. He sat up, brows pinched together, staring down at her. "What kind of witness?"

"Hey, what's the matter with you?"

"I asked you, what kind of witness?"

"I don't know. I didn't ask. And, she didn't say."

"You're not to see her again, Stella. Do you understand me? I forbid you to see Morgan Grant again. I don't want any Feds nosing around here."

"Why would the Feds—"

"They keep tabs on their witnesses, who they hang out with, could have tapped my phone."

Howie scooted off the bed, hustled to the kitchen, his heart racing as he grabbed the phone off the counter. Taking the instrument apart, he found nothing. No bug. Satisfied, he reassembled it and returned to Stella, his body suddenly filled again with tension.

He needed a smoke and Stella, in that order.

Chapter 35

THE PATTY SUE, her engine churning on low, moved slowly through the deep blue waters of the Gulf in harmony with the excited squeals of the group as another fish was hauled onto her deck. The anniversary party that had chartered the Patty Sue to celebrate the special day was having a grand old time.

Mac didn't notice. He stared at the sea ahead, sun sparking off the water hitting him in the eyes, eyes filled with Maria. The vision was so real he reached out, his fingers brushing the air, brushing the window, the glass protecting the captain on the flying bridge. His hand dropped, fingers once again gripping the wheel. He pulled the zipper up on his windbreaker, suddenly feeling a chill. January in Florida was tricky—hot in the sun, cool in the shade, and at times downright cold on the water in the breeze of a boat cutting through the waves.

This time the laughter below penetrated his mind, feeling foolish that he'd let his imagination run so wild. More gleeful screams swirled up the steps bouncing off the windows surrounding him. The case of beer the party of six brought on board for their day of fishing remained on ice in the cooler, a sure sign that the fish were running. They had shed their windbreakers in the heat building with each catch.

Mac felt Danny's presence before the elder Macintyre's elbow rubbed against him.

"Many more days like this, the word-of-mouth will push us into the best month ever. I'm thinking you'll have to buy that boat I caught you checking out in the harbor yesterday," Danny said holding out a fresh cup of coffee to his son.

"You have keen eyes, Pops. So you think it's time? Sissy's been nagging me to add another boat, too. He went on and on about how spring was around the corner and the tourists will be flocking to Anna Maria Island and Cortez. He said while I captain one boat he'd captain the other. Flo's been a big help steering business our way."

"That she has, son. Makes for a nice partnership."

A smile played over Mac's lips as he glanced at his father. Pops was approaching mid-sixties and had dropped several hints that it would be nice if Mac married, maybe have a son to keep the line going, a little Macintyre fisherman.

"So, you like Flo. Think she would make a good wife for a fisherman?" Mac asked sipping the fresh coffee.

"No one's perfect, son. I count a man lucky if he finds the love of his life … at least once … doesn't mean you're settling for second best … but, a man needs a woman to come home to. A man isn't really complete unless he has a family … a family with a child in the picture. If you know what I mean."

Mac set his mug of coffee in the holder and reached down into his pants pocket. "What do you think of this, Pops?" Mac asked holding a diamond ring between his fingers, the stone sending brilliant sparks into their eyes.

"I'd say that is a mighty fine ring you have there. Now, son, what are you going to do with it?"

"Flo and I are going to the Sandbar tonight for dinner. I'm going to ask her to marry me. I'll put this ring on her finger if she says yes. That's what I'm going to do with it," Mac said slipping the ring back into his pocket.

———

A SILVERY HALF MOON hung in the sky cradling the stars. Soft waves rolled over the warm sand receding back to the sea to form another. A January evening in Florida, a warm night, the kind that entices tourists south to escape the snow and ice up north.

It was a night for romance. A night filled with promise—stars, moon, handsome couple. The blonde woman in a sea-green wool dress walked beside the rugged fisherman, his ever present shadowy beard grazing his chin atop the white turtleneck sweater. Mac guided Flo to a table on the edge of the restaurant's patio. The legs of the white table and chairs were anchored in the soft beach sand.

The waiter set the flutes of champagne Mac requested in front of the couple, nodded, and left the lovers alone.

Flo tapped the edge of her glass to Mac's. "Cheers."

"Cheers," Mac replied.

"It's a beautiful evening, Mac. You seem a little tired. Hard day?"

"A little. It was a good day. The party you sent my way had a great time. Left with almost a hundred pounds of fish in their coolers. Pops and I thank you, Flo, for all your help."

"Well, it's mutual, you know. A man you sent to my agency a few weeks back put an offer on a house, just up the road from here. It will mean a tidy sum for me. The owners accepted his offer. I'd say we help each other—makes for a nice partnership. Don't you think?"

Mac smiled, remembering he heard the same words from Pops that afternoon. "Yeah, a nice partnership."

A woman in a floppy straw hat, the brim circled with bright red hibiscus flowers stepped out of the bushes, her eyes searching the tables. Seeing who she was looking for she made a beeline for his table. The woman bumped into Mac's arm, spilling a few drops of his champagne onto her flowered muumuu covering her ample body, a yellow-fringed scarf flowing around her neck to her hips.

"Oh, I'm so sorry, Captain Macintyre. So clumsy of me," she said plucking the white dinner napkin off the table next to Mac's knife, teetering backward as she waved the napkin open.

Looking as if she might topple over, Mac jumped up grasping her arm. "Are you all right, Crystal?"

"Yes, quite. Nice to see you." Leaning in, the woman gave Mac a hug, whispered in his ear. "Maria is alive." Straightening her hat, she smiled at Mac looking into his dark brown eyes. Turning, she nodded to Flo and then hustled away from the table disappearing in the palmetto bushes edging the side of the patio.

Mac stood staring after her as she scurried away, his heart hammering in his chest, his fingers rubbing the ring in his pocket.

"Who was that woman?" Flo asked. "You seemed to know each other."

"A crazy psychic. We met … awhile ago."

Mac returned to his seat but his eyes remained riveted on the bushes.

"Excuse me, sir. Are you ready to order?" the waiter asked.

"Ah, yes. Flo, what would you like?" Mac asked, his fingers pushing the diamond ring deep into the bottom of his pocket.

Chapter 36

THE NEWLYWEDS SNUGGLED ON the couch, a bowl of popcorn between them. The pair of private eyes were glued to the television—the latest episode of NCIS Miami. Liz, the romantic, always lit a couple of candles when they watched their shows. "Adds to the intrigue," she told Manny.

"So, Mrs. Salinas, who do you think killed the organist?"

"Well, Mr. Salinas, I'm positive it was the undercover derelict hiding in the church. Kidding aside, Mr. Salinas, wasn't our wedding the best?"

Manny looked at his bride, two weeks since their wedding day, and counted his blessings. "It was the best, Mrs. Salinas. Are you sorry we canceled our plans to be married on Anna Maria Island?"

"Maybe a little … at first. But after one bus wasn't enough, and then two couldn't handle all the guests … well, it got to be everybody else's wedding and not ours. Mom and Dad, Aunt Jane, our dogs, you and I—perfect. I still got to wear my wedding dress."

"You were a beautiful bride." Manny leaned over and gave her a smooch on the cheek.

"I thought the priest was very priestly. Didn't bat an eye when he asked for the rings in the little pouches on Maggie and Peach's collars. The dogs were so good, their tails thumping the carpet as we opened the little velvet cases. Hey, don't forget our big party for everyone in May … or June. I'm going to wear my wedding dress, you know."

They both jumped when the phone rang. Liz hit the TV's mute button as Manny picked up the receiver on the lamp table, whispering to Liz that it was Mac.

"Hey, Mac. It's two weeks late, but Happy New Year, buddy. How goes it on the west coast of Florida?"

"Manny, is Liz there?"

"Sure. Okay if I put you on speaker?"

"Absolutely."

"Hi, Mac. Happy New Year," Liz said rolling her eyes at Manny.

"Yeah, you too. First, congrats on your wedding. Sorry you had to change the location."

"Everything became verrry unwieldy, Mac. But Manny and I are extremely happy."

"I'm also sorry for calling so late but the craziest thing happened tonight. I've been stewing about what to do, if anything. I had to call you. I knew you guys would put me straight."

"Tell us, Mac," Manny said looking at his watch. Pointing to the time, he mouthed to Liz, eleven-thirty.

"I was having dinner at the Sandbar with Flo."

Liz rolled her eyes again.

"We were enjoying a drink when Crystal bumped into me. I mean literally bumped into me spilling my drink. You remember Crystal? The psychic?"

"She's hard to forget, Mac," Liz said giving Manny a peck on his cheek, along with another eye roll.

"Well, she gave me a hug, a hug that I'm sure was meant to cover up something she had to tell me."

Liz drew her legs up under her, concentrating on Mac's voice coming from the speaker phone.

"She whispered, 'Maria's alive.'"

"That's it?" Manny asked.

"Yeah. Maria's alive. It was enough to get me thinking. Off and on I've talked with my cop friend here in Cortez, quizzed him several times … was he sure Maria was killed in the crash. Yes, has always been his reply. Then I ask him about Studs and that other guy they found murdered. Do they have any leads? No, has always been that answer."

Liz and Manny locked eyes. They *knew* Maria was alive.

Manny leaned forward, elbows on his knees, head in his hands. "Mac, I don't know what to say. If your police friend—"

"I know. It's stupid. Sorry I called. Happy New Year."

"Wait, Mac. Manny and I'll do some checking … on … the Studs murder. We'll get back to you."

"Liz, I'd really appreciate that. Thanks. Bye."

"Coffee, Sherlock?" Liz asked untangling her legs while holding on to the popcorn bowl.

"Definitely calls for coffee, Watson."

Sitting at the kitchen table, the dogs, Peaches and Maggie, asleep on their big cushion beds, Liz and Manny sipped their coffee. The two candles by the television set were now on the kitchen table.

"What should we do?" Liz asked. "Mac sounded awful, but on the other hand you could tell he wanted to believe Crystal."

"We can't tell Mac," Manny said. "Something big is going down. The Feds would never have put Maria under witness protection if it wasn't big. If we say anything, we could jeopardize the case, let alone put her in danger, maybe even her life—"

"Shhh. Don't say it, Manny … that she could be killed."

"Well, she called you. I still can't believe you ID'd her in Quincy Market. Honest to God, Stitch, you are amazing." Manny leaned over, folding her hand in his. "But, when she called us on Christmas day, she said no to our calling. She has to make the move. As I said, we don't know what's happening, and she didn't want to share it with us … not at that time, anyway."

"Since when has that stopped us, Sherlock? We need information on the case."

"Well, I suppose I could call my Fed friend in Texas, the one who gave me the name of DelaCruz."

"Good. And, I suppose I could call that Fed guy. What's his name? Oh yeah, Donovan. You said Mac talked about him last summer. You have the number?"

"I'll have to look. If not, I'll call Mac."

Chapter 37

Sierra Madre Mountains, Mexico

IT WAS A COLD JANUARY day atop Junior's mountain. By a stream he dropped the reins over Devil's head, sliding off the stallion's back. Devil snorted, raised his head, and then drank from the fresh water.

Junior wrapped the fringed green, blue, red and yellow serape around his body against the chilly air. Tugging his black felt hat down further to his brows to keep the bright sun from hurting his eyes, Junior checked his cell again. Still, no text message or call from Mendoza. Junior was uneasy. Maybe Felix wasn't as clever as he thought. With the interception of the lady doctor's call to wish her mother a merry Christmas, Junior knew Dr. Maria Grayson was alive.

Mendoza had determined the call came from York, Maine, a small town near the state's southern border—tourist country, a favorite shopping destination for residents in New Hampshire and Massachusetts. Felix said he'd call as soon as he located the woman.

Junior mounted Devil, raced down the mountainside to the valley, yelling and whipping the stallion's flanks in frustration. Drawing Devil up when they reached the barn, the stallion whinnied for a treat as Junior tossed the reins to the stallion's caretaker.

Leaving the barn, Junior stalked toward his villa. On the grassy path he received the call he had been waiting for.

"I may have found the doctor," Mendoza said. "Nosing around the little town I came up with a few new residents. One caught my eye. She moved into a rental house at the time Grayson went missing. Two problems—she doesn't match the description you gave me. This woman is a blonde ... no reddish brown hair. And, she's a nurse. So I kept poking and came up with the woman's name. She's known as Morgan Grant. She works with an old timer in a family practice. Anyway, I found the rental house and decided to pay her a visit, rather pay her house a visit. I wanted to see if I could find a trace of Dr. Maria Grayson, or, better yet, if she and Morgan Grant were one and the same."

"Did you find a link between the two?" Junior asked staring out at his vast fields of marijuana. He liked the idea of the two women having the same initials. It could be a coincidence, but Junior didn't believe in coincidences.

"No, but I bugged Grant's house phone just in case. Nothing significant yet. She called a girlfriend to meet after work for a drink. I traced the number to the friend, a Stella Trent. She must have moved. By the time I arrived back in York, the phone was disconnected and the apartment she apparently rented had a for rent sign in the window. No forwarding address or phone number."

"Keep on it. As soon as you can verify that Grayson is Grant, we'll plan our next move. Get a picture with your cell of the blonde. In the meantime, find the Trent woman … ask around. Someone must know where she went."

Chapter 38

THE DELACRUZ GUN RUNNING business was picking up. For some time Junior had tried to infiltrate anti-government militia groups in the States. These groups were eager to buy untraceable weapons. Junior chuckled when the undercover project of the ATF, U.S. Bureau of Alcohol, Tobacco, Firearms and Explosives, came to light. The Bureau purposely allowed licensed firearms dealers to sell weapons to illegals hoping to track the weapons to leaders of the Mexican drug cartels. The stupid Americans let large quantities of guns cross the border from Arizona and Texas into Mexico under the guise of this project.

Junior believed he was the one bringing the U.S. agents to their knees instead. The stated goal of the ATF was to continue to track the firearms as they were transferred to higher-level traffickers and key figures in the cartels, with the expectation that this would lead to their arrests and the dismantling of the cartels, put the cartels out of business at least as far as the U.S. was concerned.

However, Junior knew that none of the targeted high-level cartel figures had been arrested. He was careful to keep at least two levels of underlings between his operation and the border guards. But the ATF scheme faltered, becoming a scandal when the U.S. Congress became aware of the project called Fast and Furious and began investigating. When the scandal broke, Junior made sure he was no longer involved with the guns crossing the border into Mexico. They were too hot. But he had to get more weapons.

Junior developed a pipeline from other dealers and refused any guns traced back to Arizona or Texas. Of special interest to the DelaCruz cartel were leaders of various militia groups in the States. A client in New England was clamoring for more weapons. He had begun to supply guns to antigovernment groups in other border states with Canada.

Mendoza told him of a Texas border guard he had met several times. The guard turned a blind eye to one of the men under Junior who smuggled guns into Texas for immediate shipment to the north. Naturally, the border guard wanted in on the money side, a cut, a generous cut of the transaction. The same border guard indicated that the gangs in the north also wanted marijuana, a purer, better grade than they were receiving through the ports of Florida and Louisiana.

The marijuana business was growing, becoming more and more lucrative for all concerned.

Junior asked Mendoza for a makeup artist. He planned to enter the U.S. from Canada. He wanted to meet this contact for himself, but did not want to reveal he was the man in charge of the cartel on the Mexican side.

The meeting became a priority for Junior. He now had two reasons for the trip: eliminate Dr. Grayson, or whatever she was calling herself these days, and to build his business with the militia—guns and the cannabis weed.

Chapter 39

Whitefield, New Hampshire

FOLLOWING JUNIOR'S ORDERS, Mendoza happily set up the meeting with his New England client—more sales meant more money for him. The meeting was to take place in Whitefield, NH, in five days. A Hollywood makeup artist, known for his character creations in horror films, was delighted at the prospect of expanding into film in Mexico. The thought of an albino as a lead character, appearing as an American until he disclosed his true intention, stimulated his creative mind. He was going to be given credit as an assistant director for the film.

Junior was enjoying the preparation for the fake film and the role he was going to play. As the lead actor he was entering the U.S. under the noses of the very organization trying to catch him.

———

AT 10:05 IN THE MORNING a white van drove up to the small Whitefield motel. The driver stepped out of the van, stretched, and sauntered into the office.

"Got a room I can crash in for a few hours? I've been on the road for eighteen. Don't want to roll into some ditch," the driver said leaning against the counter.

"You can take number three. A few hours or a night, you still have to pay for twenty-four. Sixty dollars. Cash or credit. No checks," the lady said. "You're lucky. Skiers this time of year, you know," she said taking the bills as she handed her new guest a key.

The driver ambled back to his van, parked it in front of number three, and, carrying his duffle bag, disappeared inside his room. Sitting on the edge of the bed, he snapped open his cell.

"I'm in. You going to be warm enough out there?"

"Are you kidding? As long as the meeting happens on time, doesn't last too long, I'm cozy as a piece of pie fresh from the oven with this new heater bodysuit. It would be nice if this meeting we were told about happened in unit two or four. But, I guess, that would be pressing our luck," the man in the van said.

"Yeah. I'm putting a mic in the AC vent. Remember, you have to get the pictures. I can't very well open the drapes," the driver chuckled. "There's a back door into a hallway—solid, no window, which might be a problem."

"Hold on. A car just drove up. I thought you said the meeting was scheduled for one o'clock?" van-man said.

"That was the word. Take a picture anyway," the driver said.

"It's a man. Damn."

"What's wrong?" the driver asked.

"His back is to me. Got a picture of his clothes. Never turned around. Maybe when he comes out."

"Well … where did he go?" the driver asked. "Shit."

"What?" van-man asked.

"He must have gone to his room through the hall. I heard a door close. I couldn't tell if it was next to mine. Has to be either room one or two. It's early … probably not one of the men we're waiting for."

———

THE MAKEUP ARTIST HAD done a miraculous job—face paint, wig, Western clothing. Junior chuckled at the trick he played on Mendoza when he arrived at the private airstrip in Whitefield. Mendoza had been standing at the bottom of the stairs that was rolled up to the plane's door. Stepping off the plane, Junior strolled passed Mendoza then turned, laughing. "It's me, Felix. I guess my disguise is good. I fooled you."

Mendoza turned, stared at the man for a moment, and then broke into a smile. "Beautiful. You look like a Texas oilman. That suit—tailored to your body. The black Stetson, black gloves, white scarf around your neck—wow. But your eyes, mi amigo, are those colored lenses?"

"Yes. I rather like the black," Junior said striding side-by-side with his lieutenant to the black Toyota, black tinted privacy windows.

Junior chuckled again still amused at having fooled Felix.

It was a short ride to the motel, a clean place but in need of repair.

———

AT 12:35 A BLACK Toyota parked in front of the motel's office. A man went in. A few minutes later he came out and moved his car in front of unit five.

Seeing the Toyota man park, the man in unit one quietly exited into the hallway and entered unit five.

Outside, Mendoza lifted his hand to knock on the door of unit five. The door swung open and he and Junior entered the dull yellow room, the twin beds shifted against the wall. Junior was aware, that in addition to the buyer of his weapons and perhaps some marijuana, the border guard was also going to be present. Mendoza had alerted him that the guard would not set up the meeting unless he was included. After all, he was the one whose job, and possibly his life, was on the line by letting the guns pass from Mexico to the U.S. under his not so watchful eyes.

There was a knock on the front door of unit five.

Mendoza quickly walked to take care of the intrusion. After a brief exchange, a young man bustled into the room with a serving cart. He set up a small bar on one of the scarred maple dressers, and a lunch of wrapped sandwiches, dill pickles and a taco casserole on a luggage bench. The token amenity was sent courtesy of the management for holding the meeting at their motel. One or twenty four hours, the fee for each man added up.

Felix locked the door as the young busboy left and then played the role of bartender. Easy job—four shots of whiskey.

The men had settled at a square card table. No formal introductions were asked for or given. Felix referred to Junior as a rancher who was interested in buying into the deal.

The New England buyer laid his list of guns he wanted to purchase in front of Felix who scanned the printout with his finger—an initial half-million dollar deal to see if the cartel could deliver on time. At the bottom of the list was an order for marijuana.

The meeting lasted all of thirty minutes.

The four men shook hands and parted company in different directions, leaving the sandwiches, pickles and taco casserole uneaten.

Chapter 40

DONOVAN DISCONNECTED THE CALL, his mind sparking in one direction, then another. With blood coursing through his veins, he loosened his tie, grabbed his cell off the desk and tapped Marshal Vickers' code.

"Zach, I just had the damndest call."

"Yeah? Alex, I'm—"

"Never mind what you're doing. Listen to me. Our lab at Quantico just came up with a match of a print my men found almost a year ago in Cortez, Florida. Remember those two guys I told you about when I briefed you on Morgan?"

"Vaguely. They were murdered. Those two?"

"The very ones. They were found in a dingy room by the docks, made to look like a murder suicide. It was the same night we put Dr. Maria Grayson under protection as Morgan Grant. I thought at the time the two murders were linked to DelaCruz but I could never prove it. Well, when the lab received several new prints yesterday they matched one with a print on file from those two murders. Wait, let me back up. At the time in Cortez, our forensic team found three prints—the two dead guys and a third we never could match in our database. Anyway, the Quantico lab agent just contacted me because my name was connected to the unsolved case in Cortez."

"Where did this new print come from?"

"Wait, let me check my computer. There was a meeting two days ago. ATF agents were on a stakeout. I'm expecting pictures the agents took of two men going into the meeting in Whitefield, New Hampshire."

"What was the meeting about? Why do I care?"

"A cartel running guns. Maybe drugs out of Mexico."

Zach's heel started to tap the floor. "So?"

"So? I'll tell you so. The ATF agent paid a kid to deliver a bottle of whiskey and lunch stuff to the room. When the meeting broke up, the kid pocketed the glasses left on the table. Etcetera. Etcetera. Within hours, four glasses were in our lab with PRINTS. One of the prints matched the unidentified print we had from those murders in Cortez."

Both of Zach's heels were nervously tapping the floor. "Wait. Wait. How did the ATF know about this meeting?"

"An undercover agent."

"Who? Who's this undercover agent?"

"Thaxter, Paul Thaxter."

Zach jumped to his feet. "Alex, that's the same name as Mrs. Thaxter's son—"

"What's the matter? You know him?"

"Morgan is renting the Thaxter's house. The father died and the mother is in a retirement home. She can't part with the house so she's renting it … to Morgan. Paul Thaxter was listed on the rental agreement as the contact name for the property," Zach said rubbing his scalp.

"I'll check my sources. If the undercover agent is the Paul Thaxter on the rental agreement then Morgan is right in the middle of both cases."

"We have to talk to this Paul Thaxter," Zach said pulling Morgan's file from his desk drawer.

"I agree," Donovan said.

"Wow. Did Thaxter give names? Who's he working with? Who attended the meeting?"

"Not clear. He did tell his boss that the name of the Mexican he befriended is Felix Mendoza, but the man who was attending the meeting with him was only referred to as a rancher."

"What about the other guy, the one who wanted to buy the guns? What's his name?"

"Thaxter didn't know. Mendoza only referred to him as a New England buyer. Come on, Zach. He told his ATF boss about the meeting, where, when, and the name of Mendoza."

"So, whose print was the match?" Zach asked.

"We don't know. The kid picked up four glasses. We have four sets of prints and one matches a print from the Cortez murder scene. But, there is a problem."

"Sounds like more than one," Zach said under his breath.

"The agents on the stakeout said they took pictures of three men: two went in the same room, the third disappeared in the motel's office and they only got a shot of his back. But there were four glasses on the table, and the kid said there were four men in the room when he took the booze and lunch in. Wait. I just got the pictures."

"Recognize any of them? Who do they look like? Alex, Alex."

"Hold on a second. Okay, one is definitely Mexican. One is taken from the back, no face, but his neck looks like he's a white guy—could be the New England buyer but he didn't go in the same door, and the third … damn."

"What? Who is it? What's the matter?" Zach added pencil tapping to his heel thumping.

"Too much to ask for, I guess. I hoped it was the albino, but it can't be. Doesn't look like him. The man in the picture is definitely dark skinned and the eyes, well, let's just say they're not pink. Must be he's the rancher Thaxter mentioned. No name."

"Well, Alex. The print matches one of those guys. One of them is a killer."

"You're right. Look at the big picture—we have a missing piece of a puzzle," Alex said. "It may or may not have anything to do with Junior DelaCruz and your witness. The ATF guys have been working the case from the bottom up and we're concentrating on the top guy. Their database didn't hook up with ours until now. I'll talk to Thaxter."

Chapter 41

DONOVAN'S VOICE WAS STRANGLED with frustration as he paced around his office, the phone to his ear. "Thaxter, you have to give me more. At the meeting—a Mexican by the name of Felix Mendoza, a rancher and a white guy from New England. Who else? Names? Come on, Thaxter, their names."

"I don't know. There were those three. There weren't four."

"What do you mean you don't know? And, how do you come up with three guys. There were four glasses."

"I ... I don't know. Get off my back, Donovan."

"You've been undercover for almost a year and all you can give me is the name of some Mexican?"

"I said, GET OFF MY CASE. Talk to my boss. I gave him the tip that there was going to be a meeting regarding a gun buy, the time and place of the meeting, and the name of my contact who gave me the information."

Donovan stood. Fuming. Thaxter had hung up the phone.

Hands on his head, fingers laced, Donovan paced. Digging into his pants for his cell he hit Zach's number.

"I talked to Thaxter."

"And?" Zach said

"*And*, he insists there were only three at the meeting, *and* that he only has one name, *and* to talk to his boss if I don't like what he had to say."

"Nice. Thaxter's boss must be happy. He's making progress on his gun runners and we're still running on empty as far as the albino goes. I'll tell Morgan about the fingerprints, but we don't know what it means. Maybe nothing new in her case."

As Zach talked, Donovan added a name to the case board, pressed the save button, and sent the file to Zach along with the pictures of three men—two who attended the meeting.

"You said the ATF agents, who staked out the meeting, only got pictures of these three you just sent me? One of them is from the back. Hardly an easy person to ID." Zach said his finger rolling the mouse wheel several times. And they didn't see him go into the same room as the other two. So, he may not have been involved."

Case: DelaCruz Cartel		
<u>Target</u>: Junior DelaCruz, missing <u>Crime</u>: Murder, Gun Running, Drugs <u>Last seen</u>: Anna Maria Island, FL, 6 months ago	<u>Believed he killed:</u> √Perez Studs Wally	<u>Known Bugs</u> Mother-2 Mac-2 Morgan-3
Felix Mendoza Rancher & white guy?		
—	—	▪ ▪ ▪

"That's what I'm told. One more thing. The agent inside said he heard a door close in the hallway at the time the man disappeared in the office. What do you think?"

"Thaxter's lying. I think he's a double agent."

Chapter 42

A FINGERPRINT? A fingerprint matching a print at the Cortez murder scene? Could it be a break? Whose print?

Morgan mulled over Zach's call, his words. Could it mean she was going back to her own life soon? But without Mac as part of her life ... was that what she wanted? To go back to what?

More questions crept in, circled in her mind.

It wasn't what Zach had told her, but she wondered if he was holding something back. She had never heard the name Felix Mendoza, and then there was the rancher? If Mendoza was a Mexican, who was the rancher? Did they leave the States together after the meeting? Did they go back to Mexico? Zach said the picture didn't match the albino but then she didn't match Dr. Maria Grayson either.

Zach had dismissed the information about the gun running cartel Thaxter had infiltrated. There were many Mexican cartels—pitting one against the other seemed to be the game of the day—kill each other off—the ultimate power grab. She was aware that Paul Thaxter was a border guard but could he really be an undercover agent? That would be good, or was he a double agent? And who were the other men at that meeting? Zach only talked about the meeting in passing, saying it didn't really have anything to do with her case.

So many questions. Zach said he was on his way to York. Maybe he would have more answers for her.

A tinge of fear wormed slowly through her bones sending a chill up her arms. Someone was watching her. She was sure of it. She glanced at the kitchen window, then the living room windows—black glass, seeing only her reflection.

"Nerves. I'm getting jumpy. Come on, Jenny, time to go on our nightly patrol. Let's check the house. Make sure it's buttoned up tight."

With Jenny at her side Morgan checked all the doors, all the windows pulling the shades closed, and then climbed the stairs to her bedroom. Retrieving her revolver from the nightstand, she checked the chamber. It was loaded. She sat down in Mrs. Thaxter's rocking chair, tapping her foot on the floor, rocking in a slow rhythm as she looked at the ceiling. *Come on, Morgan, get a grip,* she thought trying to regain her composure. Deep breathing wasn't helping. *A glass of wine, yes, that's the ticket while I wait for Zach.*

Pointing the gun to the ceiling, she gripped the handrail with her free hand and hustled down to the kitchen. Uncorking the half-full bottle of wine, her heart skipped a beat. Was that a noise or her nerves playing tricks?

She waited.

There, another noise. Jenny cocked her head, whined and scampered into the living room.

Morgan waited.

Jenny trotted back and sat by her side, tongue hanging out. Morgan patted her head and began pouring the wine into the glass.

Another noise.

Morgan froze, wine bottle in the air, head tilted, concentrating. What was it?

Zach had a key.

The sound wasn't of a key turning in the lock. Besides Zach knew she was home. He would have knocked, called out and entered.

Another sound.

A tap on the living room window?

Glass shattered.

"Jenny," she whispered. "Come."

Leaving the wine goblet on the counter she raced to the computer room, lifted the trapdoor, grabbed the flashlight she kept at the top of the stairs, and closed the door above her as she and Jenny stepped down into the cellar.

Hearing footsteps overhead she and Jenny backed into the corner of the stone-faced cellar. She switched off the flashlight. The cellar was pitch black.

"Ms. Grant, I know you're here. Come out so we can talk. Don't be afraid."

Morgan pressed her back against the cold stone clutching Jenny's collar.

She didn't recognize the voice. Seemed muffled.

"Don't think you can hide. Too bad, I guess you aren't going to come out."

Footsteps.

More footsteps—computer room, kitchen, back to the computer room. The trapdoor opened. A slash of light fell on the stairs, fell across the cement floor in front of Morgan. "If you don't come out I'll have to come get you."

A gun shot rang out ricocheting off the stone. "If you don't come out willingly then I'm afraid I'll have to come for you. That would not be pretty."

Morgan saw a foot take the first step, then a second, a third … five more. With only the light through the trapdoor, she could see he was dressed all in black, a white scarf around his neck. She couldn't see his face in the shadow of his large black hat. The slash of light fell on metal, shiny metal, gun metal … in his hand.

"Stay, Jenny," she whispered.

Breathing deep, steadying her nerves, willing her hand not to shake, Morgan held out the revolver with both hands as the man stepped onto the cement shooting into the blackness. The bullet was close nicking a piece of granite stone to her right.

Morgan aimed at the man silhouetted in the light of the open trapdoor.

Another shot rang out hitting the floor in front of her.

Morgan pulled the trigger.

The man shot again in the air as he fell backward.

Jenny barked breaking from Morgan's side. This time her growl was real, fierce. Guttural growls mixed with snarls.

"Morgan, where are you. Are you down there? I heard a shot."

"Zach?"

"Yes. I'm coming."

Zach started down the steep stairs, gun drawn.

Morgan remained pressed again the granite wall, watching the man coming down the stairs, waiting, making sure it was really Zach. He stepped onto the cement. "Morgan?"

Morgan turned on her flashlight, aiming the beam on the floor in front of her. Jenny whined racing back to her side.

Zach looked down at the body lying on the floor, a gun near his hand. Zach kicked the gun to the side, bent down checking for a pulse. "He's dead, Morgan," he said striding to her, his arms open as she slumped against him, her fingers still clutching, frozen to the gun.

"Are you all right?" he asked holding her from collapsing onto the floor. Her body trembled against him.

"I shot him, Zach."

Zach pulled a handkerchief from his pocket. "Give me the gun. It's okay," he said wrapping the cloth around the weapon in Morgan's hand. He led her passed the legs of the body, up the stairs to the living room, to the couch.

"Stay here, I'll go down to see if I can ID him."

Morgan sat, letting her head drop to the back of the couch. Jenny, panting, leaned against her.

Zach returned to the living room, cell to his ear, then slipped it back on his belt. Squatting in front of Morgan, he took hold of her hands.

"He's really dead?" she asked.

"Yes. I called Donovan. He's sending an agent to pick up the body. He wants to keep it quiet. No local police. No press."

"Did you look under his shirt, see his ghostly albino skin?"

"The man isn't an albino. He's not DelaCruz."

"I don't understand." Morgan lifted her head from the back of the couch. "Who is it?"

"Paul Thaxter."

Chapter 43

THAXTER DEAD? Morgan shot him? Shot him because he was shooting at her? Donovan stared at his cell lying on his desk.

Snatching the phone he hit the code for his ATF contact. Before the man could identify himself, Donovan started yelling. "What the hell is going on? Your man just tried to kill my witness. But guess what?"

"Donovan calm down. What are you talking about?"

"Your border guard Paul Thaxter. He's dead. Morgan Grant, my witness, killed him because he tried to kill her. That's what I'm talking about."

"Dammit! We had suspicions he might be a double agent. You may have just confirmed those suspicions. I was going to call you."

"Oh, yeah. How convenient I happened to call you."

"Don't get testy, Donovan. Those prints on the glasses. Interesting that Thaxter turns up dead. His prints were on one of those glasses. Matched his prints in his personnel file, yet he swore he wasn't at the meeting. So now we have three matches. Two names. One matched the print at the Cortez scene. We don't know who that is. The other two—Thaxter and Felix Mendoza. Thaxter sent us a shot glass with Mendoza's print when he first infiltrated the cartel. He hoped that Mendoza would lead him to his boss, or his boss's boss, up the chain to DelaCruz or another gang. I guess Thaxter had a change of heart as to whose side he was on. The fourth print, the rancher guy, may be DelaCruz. We don't know and they all slipped away. Vanished. Now, you have Paul Thaxter dead. I sent you the pictures. Given Thaxter was after your witness our cases seem to be tied together at the hip."

Donovan sighed. "Yeah, I guess you can say that. I sent an agent to pick up Thaxter's body, keeping this quiet, no local police. I'm going up to York to meet with my U.S. Marshal and the witness. For God's sake, please keep in touch."

Chapter 44

———

Portsmouth, NH

BOND WAS ECSTATIC. The meeting with Felix Mendoza had gone better than he expected.

Leaving the motel that afternoon, he stopped at a bar, had a few drinks. Feeling no pain, he didn't drive home that night preferring to celebrate his success with one of the bar's waitresses.

The next morning, he wasn't in a hurry to leave, had breakfast as he kept playing the meeting over in his mind. The rancher didn't say anything. He only watched. But every time Mendoza had to make a decision, to agree or disagree with Bond's request, Felix looked at the rancher, the rancher signaled—touching his ear, other movements such as raising his pinky finger. Bond knew the rancher was in charge.

Whatever the code, Howie's shipment of guns would be delivered in seven days, separated into five wooden cases. The cases were to be delivered to a storage locker in Portsmouth. Bond was to take possession of the crates in person or the crates would be returned to the sender.

There was no agreement, hence no deal, on including marijuana in this shipment—maybe in the future, maybe in a month.

Howie finally decided to head home. He had work to do and he still had several hours of driving time. Turning the key in the ignition he was rewarded with a clicking sound. He tried again. Same thing. "Damn battery. I should have gone straight home, now I have to find a repair shop."

With the delay in replacing his battery, and stopping for dinner to see the waitress again, he didn't get home until almost ten o'clock. He tiptoed in hoping he didn't have to deal with Stella. He had to make some calls. He was in luck. Everything was quiet, only the hall light was on.

While Stella slept in the bedroom, the door closed for privacy, Bond alerted his buyers in Michigan and Wisconsin that they should be ready to pick up their share of the shipment when Howie had possession of the crates. Each buyer was to rent a black van. Bond would meet them at the storage facility. He would send an email confirming the time and address.

His business done, Howie turned off the light. He was ready for a romp with Stella. He was tired but his body remained tightly wired. Reaching for the doorknob the door gave way. Strange. He had purposely shut the door so Stella wouldn't hear his conversations.

Howie climbed into bed, snuggling around Stella, pulling her close, drawing her hair back on her neck, nibbling her ear.

"Howie?"

"Yeah, it's me baby. I thought you were asleep."

"Howie, I'm going with you." She didn't answer in her sleepy voice. Did she overhear his telephone calls?

"Where?"

"The storage locker." She turned to him her lips full, soft, her hand running over his body. "Howie, you can trust me ... your business. I'll help."

"No, Stella. I don't want you to worry your pretty—"

"My pretty little head is full of brains, Howie. I know what you're doing. Now make love to me, you know you want to. You're ready."

Furious with himself for being so careless, furious with Stella for intruding into his life, he released his tensions, quick and hard, Stella whimpering. She lay crying into her pillow as he promised to end her pain. He left her naked on the rumpled bed sheets, curled in a fetal ball. He returned moments later jamming a needle between her toes on her left foot. She cried out then immediately fell still, eyes closed.

———

AROUND 2 A.M. A SQUAD CAR, patrolling an abandoned section of town saw what looked to be a person on a snow bank partially hidden by a dumpster. The officer and his partner hurried to the body of a woman. The driver called dispatch relaying what they had found as his partner checked the woman's vital signs. "Hey, she's alive. Tell dispatch to get an ambulance here fast."

The woman tried to say something but the second officer couldn't make out the words. She bent closer. Was it a name? Doctor something?

The ambulance, siren blaring, red light whirling, pulled up next to the victim, the medics quickly transferring her to the van, sped away to the hospital.

The hospital's emergency team immediately began administering to the woman. In and out of consciousness, the woman continued to mouth something but it was inaudible. Finally with great effort, she cried out for Dr. Grant.

A nurse stepped to the wall phone. "Our patient is asking for a Dr. Grant. Anyone by that name on staff?"

"Hang on, let me check. I don't see a Grant here. Let me check the other hospitals in Portsmouth ... sorry, nothing."

"Maybe someone dumped her here ... over the border. She could be an attempted murder victim. Check York Hospital. They have sister hospitals in all the border towns. Call me back, I'm in the ER."

The woman on night duty at the York Hospital information desk, laid down the latest issue of *Cooking Light*, and answered the phone. Finally someone needed her help.

The caller identified herself. She was calling from a hospital in Portsmouth. A patient had just been brought in, critical condition, asking for a Dr. Grant. Did the night duty attendant know of a doctor by that name?

The attendant pulled up a search for all doctors affiliated with the hospital and the satellites. "No. There's no Dr. Grant listed on our staff, but the name ... my doctor, Dr. Farnsworth, has a nurse practitioner. Her name is Grant, Morgan Grant."

A few minutes later a call roused Morgan from bed. The caller informed her that a woman seemed to have been left for dead on a snow bank in Portsmouth and was asking for a Dr. Grant. "You're a nurse, but—"

"Wait, I'm Dr. Grant. Do you have her name? A description?"

"Let me transfer you to the ER."

"Hello, Dr. Grant. I don't know if you are the one this woman is asking for, her voice is faint."

"What's the matter with her?"

"No injuries … looks like a drug overdose."

"Ask her if her name is Stella, Stella Trent. I'll hold."

Morgan could hear muffled voices, picturing the Emergency Room scene, a domain she knew well.

"Dr. Grant, the woman nodded her head. Hold on, I'm going to put the receiver to her ear … okay, talk." The ER nurse held the phone to Stella's ear.

"Stel, it's Morgan."

"Mo?" her voice was faint.

"Yes. Who did this to you? Was it Howard, Stel? Did he try to kill you?"

"Yes … he's wor … he's working with Paul …" The voice trailed off.

"Paul who?"

"Thax. Mo … be … care …"

"Sorry, Dr. Grant. She has no more strength. Perhaps in another hour."

Morgan thanked the nurse and closed her cell. She hustled down the stairs. Maybe Zach was awake. He had insisted he was staying with her until he and Donovan came up with a plan on how to handle Thaxter's death.

Finding Zach at the kitchen table, she relayed her conversation with the Portsmouth hospital and Stella's condition. "I won't be able to go back to sleep. Coffee?"

"Sounds good. I presume you want to go to Portsmouth … pick up Stella?" Zach said.

"Now you're a mind reader. That's exactly what I want to do. From what I could tell she didn't have any injuries. No bleeding. Which tells me Howard Bond drugged her. With antidotes the ER doctor is administering, they should be able to bring her around quickly. That's not to say she doesn't need help, but I can take care of her here. Zach. I think she's in danger."

"Well, there's so much new information, we can't start putting everything together until Donovan gets here. If we're going to drive to Portsmouth and back, we should leave here by nine o'clock."

"I agree," Morgan said putting out sugar packets, creamer carton, and mugs. "My nerves are frazzled. I always feel someone is watching me, stalking. The feeling raises the hair on my neck. Yesterday proved my instincts were right. Thaxter was stalking me."

Zach poured the coffee and they both slumped down on the kitchen chairs. Morgan looked at Jenny, asleep on her braided rug, twitching.

"Look at Jenny. Gun shots, dead guy in the cellar … don't tell me animals aren't affected by what's going on around them."

Zach gazed at Morgan. "Donovan's agent picked up the body about an hour ago. You slept through it. I told them to be quiet. It was quick." Taking a sip of coffee, he continued to look at Morgan. "What will you do if Donovan gets DelaCruz?"

"What do you mean, what will I do?"

"You know … go back to your other life … Florida, a surgeon … the fisherman?"

"Zach, I've dreamed of ending this. I wrote Mac letters. Don't panic, I didn't mail them. But, you know that PI who ID'd me? Well, I called her, wished her a merry Christmas. She thought you and me … when she saw us at Quincy Market in Boston, that you and I—"

"You and me? That's really out there. Don't you—"

"Yes, Zach. That would be out there." Morgan's eyes locked with his. She wanted him to understand the two of them, together, was not going to happen.

"But then there's that doctor … New Year's Eve. You went to Moosehead Lake," Zach said.

"Yeah."

"So, we're full circle to … what will you do? Go back?" he asked.

"Oh, I want to go back but it will be a different life. I've lost him."

"Hey, hey, did he tell you that? I'm presuming you're talking about the fisherman," Zach asked walking to the counter for a tissue. God, he didn't want to make her cry.

"No, but he thinks I'm dead. And, Liz, the PI, said something … like maybe Mac had a new girlfriend. No, more than that. Probably a lover."

"So, you have to tell him. Of course, the sight of a ghost could kill him."

That brought a smile to her lips as she continued dabbing her tears.

Chapter 45

Port Orange, Florida

FEBRUARY FIRST. A new month.

Manny sat staring into his morning coffee.

Liz sat staring at Manny with her big brown eyes. "You told Mac you'd check around. How are you going to do that?" she asked, dabbing a drop of orange marmalade off her white-cotton nightshirt sprinkled with black and brown puppies, her springy red curls dancing with each dab.

Manny looked up. He adored Liz. How lucky can a guy get? "There you go, Stitch. Straight to the point," he said with a sigh.

"She's alive, Manny. We can't just sit here. You, we have to … have to nudge things along."

"You mean we have to meddle."

"This is much bigger than a little meddle thingy. Mac's our friend. We have to get involved."

Manny reached for his cell propped up on the cream carton.

"Who're you calling?"

"My officer friend in Texas. The one I called when Mac first told us Maria's story. The guy who told me about DelaCruz. I talked to him a few weeks ago after Mac called, but he didn't have anything new to add. I'll try again."

While Manny talked on the phone, Liz put their cereal bowls in the dishwasher. Let the dogs out. Let the dogs in. Topped off the coffee mugs then sat as Manny said goodbye.

"Well, that was interesting," he said taking a sip of the hot coffee.

"Come on, Sherlock, tell me what he said. That conversation was longer than hello, how are you, and so long."

"He said they still can't find DelaCruz. Then, he went on to say that one of their border guards who had infiltrated the cartel was potentially a double agent, emphasis on potentially. This double-agent guy was shot a couple of days ago. Killed."

"Where? Texas?"

"No. York, Maine, of all places. Two cities—York and Boston—can't be more than an hour one way or the other. Sounds like it could fit with Maria but—"

"My instincts exactly—border guards, DelaCruz, we see Maria in Boston. Scrabble. But what do we do about it?" Liz said, both hands around her mug leaning in, her eyes squinting at Manny.

"I think it's time I call that Fed guy Mac told us about, what's-his-name?" Manny asked.

"Donovan. Mac gave you his number. I tried him when you called your Texas contact before. He wouldn't talk to me." Liz said scrolling the directory of her cell. "Here, you call. I'll get the Atlas. Just want to make sure of the distances. Tell Donovan that the three of us are coming to Boston."

"Three?"

"Come on, Sherlock. I think it's time we bring Mac into the conversation. Depending on what Donovan has to say, of course."

———

"DONOVAN HERE."

"Hi, Agent Donovan. You may not know me. My name is Manny Salinas. My partner, Elizabeth Stitchway, and I are good friends of Mac Macintyre and Maria Grayson. We're private investigators."

Liz nodded rapidly, urging her husband on.

Manny raised his brows, nodding. "I'm calling you about the Dr. Maria Grayson case."

"What makes you think I'm working such a case?"

"My partner and I were in Boston a few months back," Manny said ignoring the agent's question.

"Yeah?"

"Yeah. We saw Maria in Quincy Market. I said to Elizabeth at the time that I bet she's being handled by that Agent Donovan's Boston Field Office. We thought the three of us, Elizabeth and I and Mac might take a trip to Boston. You remember Mac don't you? Mac Macintyre, the fisherman from Cortez, Florida?"

"Why would you do that?" Donovan's remark was sharp, cryptic.

"Well, being we think Maria is alive, we thought we'd start our search in Boston. By the way, Mac also thinks she's alive."

"If there was such a case, and I'm not saying there is, why would he think such a person is alive?"

"A psychic told him." Manny rolled his eyes at Liz as she tried, unsuccessfully, to stifle a laugh.

"Come on, a psychic?"

"Well, the psychic along with our sighting. Dr. Grayson was having coffee in one of those outdoor cafes that are so popular in Boston. She was with a good looking bald guy."

"Zach," Donovan whispered, more to himself than to his caller. "All of this is crazy. You can't be sure."

"Oh, yes we can. Maria called us … Christmas day."

"Look, Mr. PI Salinas, some of my cases are beginning to pop. If what you say is true, and mind you I'm not saying it is, I can't have you meddling. I don't have time—"

"Meddle? We don't want to meddle," Manny again rolled his eyes at Liz who had to leave the table unable to hold back the laugh that erupted. "Let us help. Two private investigators for the price of one—pro bono—no charge."

Liz scurried back to the table her head bobbing up and down like a bobble-head doll.

"Let me think about it?"

"Okay, but we're going to have a chat with Mac. We'll tell him about Boston."

Liz pressed her ear to Manny's ear.

"She's not in Boston."

"I figured. Where is she?"

"That's classified … for now."

The call was disconnected.

"Emanuel Salinas, you are magnificent. Donovan just confirmed Dr. Maria Grayson is in fact alive."

Chapter 46

Cortez, Florida

HIGH NOON. SUN BEATING down in a cloudless sky. Anyone fishing out on the Gulf was slathered with sunscreen, the higher the potency the better. Mac kept the Patty Sue on a slow idle. The fish were running and the party of seven that chartered the excursion had no thoughts of stopping for a lunch break, not while they were hauling in red snapper fish-over-reel in the invigorating, salty sea air.

Danny laughed as he climbed up to the flying bridge with a fresh mug of coffee and a ham and cheese on rye sandwich for his son. Golly gee, but he loved playing host without all the responsibilities of caring for the boat or the business.

Mac waved off the ham and cheese but gratefully thanked his pops for the coffee as his cell rang. Seeing it was Manny he quickly pushed the cell to his ear. "Manny, any news?"

"Hi, Mac. Liz is on the speaker. Saw the weather report—must be a beautiful day for fishing."

"It is. News, Manny. Any news?"

"Hi, Mac. It's Liz. We have all kinds of stuff to tell you."

"Give it to me," Mac said biting his lip.

"I just got off the phone with Agent Donovan," Manny said.

"What did he have to say?" Mac motioned to his pops to take over the wheel.

"I don't know if you're ready for this," Liz said. "You tell him, Manny."

"Maria is alive."

Mac's heart stopped. Slowly he sucked in some air letting Manny's words sink in, pulling his fingers through his black wavy hair. "Damn!" Mac swore as his coffee trickled down his white shirt, landing on his white boat shoes.

Danny tore off a sheet of paper towel, handed it to his son, taking the empty mug from him. Danny squinted at Mac. The boy's fingers were shaking.

"Mac. Did you hear me, Mac? Maria's alive," Manny said.

"I heard you," he whispered. "Give me a minute … I spilled my coffee." Swiping the paper towel across his shirt and pants, he put the towel to his face swiping at the tear in his eye, and several that followed.

"Is she all right?" His words caught in his throat.

"Seems to be," Manny said.

"Where is she?"

"Somewhere in or near Boston, as far as we can tell," Manny said.

"Mac, please don't get mad at us," Liz said. "We saw her—"

"I wasn't sure at all that it was Maria," Manny chimed in. "But Stitch was sure. Wrote a note on her business card which we gave to a waitress … we were in Quincy Market, Boston, having coffee … several months ago."

"My God, did you talk to her?"

"No way, Mac," Liz said. "We would never blow her cover. And besides, like Manny said, my gut feeling could have been wrong. It happens once in awhile … the gut thing."

"But you talked to Donovan. He confirmed she's alive? He must know where she is. I have to go … now," Mac turned to his dad. "Pops, check when the next flight out of Orlando to—"

"Wait, Mac. You, we can't go. Not yet. She's a witness … a protected witness. Donovan really didn't want to tell us anything. But he did say things were popping, his words, at least we think he was referring to Maria's case. I don't know how long it will take him to wrap it up, but I'm hopeful it will be soon."

"Mac," Liz said in a soft voice, "We don't know what soon means. We want to go with you. We'll keep in touch. I promise."

Chapter 47

York, Maine

BARLY PINNED MORGAN against the wall, pushing the examination room door shut with his foot. "Why won't you answer my calls?" His voice was stressed, full of frustration, but controlled.

"I ..."

"I what? It's been four weeks, Morgan. Not a word. No explanation. One minute we're having a wonderful time, midnight and—"

"Don't say any more," Morgan said putting her fingers on his lips to stop him from painting the picture, the picture so vivid in both their minds, the picture of his making love to her in front of the fireplace. Her heart began to thump. How was she going to explain? There was no way. She knew he could feel her skin warming to his touch. *Stop it, Morgan.*

Suddenly his lips were on hers, strong, wanting her.

Wriggling free of his grip, she leaned against the door smoothing the flowered scrubs over her skirt. "Barly, I told you, it was a mistake. I'm involved—"

"Involved? With whom? I haven't seen anyone hanging around. Who—"

"Not a who. I mean ... Barly, I'm involved in a situation. I can't explain now. Maybe soon. But, you and I, it shouldn't have happened. It was New Year's Eve, the champagne, I wanted ... it was a mistake."

Chapter 48

Portland, Maine

"NO, FELIX. IF WE'RE going to trust Howard Bond, he has to prove himself. If he wants to be our main distributor to the U.S. militia groups, he must do away with Maria Grayson. He has to be the one to pull the trigger."

"Sí, I agree, Señor. We don't have many choices. Fact is, Bond is our only choice. Thaxter kept a tight control on Bond. Now Thaxter's disappeared, so Bond is demanding to take the position Thaxter held. Bond wants his piece of the pie. He's very ambitious, wants all the action, taking orders only from me, which, of course, means taking your orders, Señor."

"Strange how Thaxter suddenly vanished. He talked like a dedicated lieutenant at our meeting in Whitefield. Do you suppose he was playing us, Felix?"

"Could have been, but I didn't witness any evidence of it. And you know, I'm always checking our sources."

"You're a fine man, Felix. Your suggestion to stay close to the Grayson woman until she is no longer a threat was wise. Portland has many people, enough so that we can move about as strangers without arousing suspicion, yet close to Grayson to make sure she's taken care of."

"Too bad, Señor, that Thaxter disappeared without taking *care* of her, didn't follow through on his assignment, your test of loyalty, as he pledged to do."

"Just as well we found out now that he couldn't be trusted. Never again, Felix. We left ourselves exposed. Once we see if Bond passes the test you must immediately recruit another distributor, maybe more, in the northern states of the U.S. Do you understand me, Felix?"

"Sí, I understand."

"Good. Now call Bond back. Thank him for alerting us to Thaxter's disappearance. Tell him about the test. Tell him if he wants to join us, he must first prove his loyalty. Grayson and the Feds are keeping quiet. I'm not sure why, but they must be planning something. All the more reason we test Bond. If he doesn't pass, then we have to find someone else who can give us information on the elusive Maria Grayson, otherwise known as Morgan Grant. Felix, you may have to take up residency in York. You're looking a little pale. Definitely in need of a doctor." Junior chuckled at the thought of the Mexican looking pale.

"We can tell Bond that Thaxter obviously did not pass the test as he left the job undone. Maybe he was careless, underestimated the wily Morgan Grant, and fled, or worse, he's a double agent as you suggested, in which case, we must find him, eliminate him as well," Felix said.

"When you talk to Bond tell him to send me a picture of Morgan Grant. You sent me one, but I want another, see if she's changed her disguise. Tell him we will be traveling to Portsmouth soon to have a chat."

"I'll call him now, Señor. He will be surprised that we are so close, that you didn't return to Mexico after the meeting."

"Good. I like to keep him off balance about my whereabouts. We'll have a smoke, a shot of tequila together, plan how we want Bond to fulfill his agreement, provided he agrees," Junior said.

"Oh, he'll agree, Señor. He's hungry for money and power."

Mendoza was quick to follow his boss's order. Picking up his cell, he punched Bond's number.

"Howard, Felix Mendoza here."

"Felix. How are you? Good to hear from you."

"I wonder, Howard, any word from Paul Thaxter?"

"No. Felix, if you're calling to tell me my next shipment is delayed—"

"No, no, mi amigo. Nothing like that. Thaxter's disappearance has left a hole in our organization, duties that must be carried out or there will be no expansion into the States. I have a proposition for you." Felix smiled at Junior. A little pressure might force Bond to make a quick decision.

Felix filled Howard in on how he must prove himself. Then he sprang Junior's offer, provided Howard agreed to the terms.

Bond didn't hesitate. He agreed to the terms—eliminate Morgan Grant and in return he would be the sole distributor to all the militia groups he could line up.

Ending the conversation, Felix joined Junior, the two men sat in comfy chairs across the glass coffee table in their hotel suite. Felix lit up the rolled cigarette on the silver tray beside the crystal shot glasses. "Bond agreed to your terms, Señor," he said pouring the clear liquor.

The two men raised their glasses to each other and inhaled a long draw through their purest weed, savoring it, slowly releasing the smoke through parted lips.

"We have to have an escape plan, Felix. We will witness Bond's actions from a distance but close enough to be sure he passes the test. Then we'll leave. But, if things go awry, in case Bond sets a trap for us, we must have options to get away. Road and airports would be watched. Some other means of travel will be required."

"Sí, Señor. I will take care of it."

Chapter 49

———

York, Maine

DONOVAN TURNED HIS GREEN Ford rental car into Morgan's driveway, parked behind a black SUV, and slid out from behind the wheel. Standing a moment, he glanced around at the snow covered grounds—barren trees, except for the pines, and a few evergreen philodendrons. His gaze stopped on a garden shed to the left of the garage. Turning, he looked at the split-rail fence between the house and the street—no bushes to hide behind.

Stomping his feet on the driveway testing the ice underfoot, he leaned back into the car to retrieve his laptop and briefcase and slowly walked up to the house. Zach was standing behind the front storm door, arms crossed, waiting for the agent. Without a word Zach opened the door, and from Donovan's outstretched hands took the laptop and briefcase placing them inside next to a lamp table.

Zach stepped outside, letting the storm door shut behind him. The agent and the U.S. Marshal, both dressed in black—parka, turtleneck sweater, trousers, boots—began their trek around the house. They took note of the animal paw prints including Jenny's where she had chased a rabbit, a squirrel, or other woodland creature.

From time to time a remark passed from one to the other, one of which was the absence of any human footprints. As of yet, no one had been stalking around the house. Donovan pointed to the shed, the size of a large garage. He wanted to look inside.

An open padlock hung from the hasp. Zach pocketed the lock and pushed on the door. One small window filled the shed with dim light. The Thaxters had obviously emptied the contents of the shed—sold off or sent to the junkyard. The two exceptions: a riding lawn mower and a snow shovel. Donovan set the shovel outside the shed, leaning it next to the door, a simple explanation for the footprints, if anyone was looking.

Stepping back into the shed he flipped the light switch. A bulb in the center of the ceiling responded adding more illumination. A workbench stood against the left wall with an electric power strip mounted above. Donovan smiled, there was plenty of room and electrical power for his SWAT team.

Hands on hips, he turned to Zach. "You picked up Stella Trent?"

"Yeah."

"Is she cooperating?" Donovan asked.

"So far. Her so-called lover tried to kill her," Zach said.

"Okay, I've seen enough." The two men left the shed. Zach inserted a stick through the hasp to secure the door, keeping the padlock in his pocket.

Entering the living room, Morgan acknowledged Donovan, inviting them into the kitchen where Mr. Coffee was brewing a fresh pot.

Zach introduced Donovan to Stella bundled in a blanket, sitting at the kitchen table with her feet up on a stool.

Donovan set his laptop on the table and sat down, leaning his briefcase on the floor against the chair. "I have a few photos to show you ladies. Tell me if you recognize anyone," he said turning the laptop so they could both see the screen.

Two men, a black car behind them, appeared to be walking up to a door. It was the picture the ATF agents took on their stakeout at the Whitefield motel.

"Do you recognize either of these men?"

Stella shook her head.

Donovan looked at Morgan. She was leaning forward scrutinizing the screen. "Can you zoom in on the guy on the right?" she asked squinting.

"Sure," Donovan said. "Take your time."

"No, I've never seen either one."

"Okay, how about this one?"

"It's Howie." Stella's feet dropped to the floor, her hand covering her mouth in disbelief. "That's his jacket. Where was this taken? What was he doing?" Her words came in a whisper.

"Whitefield, New Hampshire. Less than a week ago. Are you sure it's him? Only the man's back—"

"I know because of the snag on the shoulder. See." Stella leaned on the table, her finger touching the screen, touching the raveled thread on Howie's jacket.

"Were you aware he was going to Whitefield?" Donovan asked.

"He said he had business in Whitefield. He was gone a couple of days, but I don't know why."

Morgan put her arm around her friend. She could see that Stella was conflicted, in denial similar to a battered wife syndrome. Stella had become a liability when she told Howie she wanted in on his business.

"What do you think he was doing, Stella?" Donovan asked quietly but with a force that he wanted her to answer.

"He was a day-trader." Stella looked from the agent to the marshal to Morgan. Fear in her eyes. She felt trapped, cornered.

"What else was he involved in?" Donovan asked, this time his voice was strong, demanding.

Stella broke into tears, covering her face. "I think … I think … I think guns. He was buying and selling guns." She stumbled from the kitchen, falling onto the couch in a ball, sobbing, deep racking sobs.

Morgan went to her friend, covered her with another blanket, smoothing her hair back from her eyes. "I'll be in the kitchen, Stel. Try to rest."

Chapter 50

IT WAS TIME TO READ Morgan into the script. Donovan looked up from his computer screen.

"Morgan this is how we're going to lure Bond, Mendoza, and the rancher here, to this house. Please bring Stella back here if she's able. She has become a player."

Case: DelaCruz Cartel

Target: Junior DelaCruz, missing	**Believed he**	**Known**
Crime: Murder, Gun Running, Drugs	**killed:**	**Bugs**
Last seen: Anna Maria Island, FL, 7	√Perez	Mother-2
months ago	√Studs	Mac-2
	√Wally	Morgan-3
Persons of Interest		
Felix Mendoza, Rancher, Howard Bond		
Paul Thaxter: dead		

Donovan updated the case board replacing *white guy* with Howard Bond, adding Paul Thaxter. With the unidentified print from the double murder in Cortez matching a print on the glass from the meeting at the Whitefield motel, and with the rancher the only person unaccounted for, Donovan believed he could start to make the case that the rancher was DelaCruz, the man who killed not only Perez, but Studs and Wally. Hopefully he could prove this by catching him in SWAT's net.

Completing his updates, he turned off the computer and faced Morgan and Stella sitting by her side. The sobs had stopped, her red eyes still shedding an occasional tear.

"The lure, dangling me as bait. Tell me who's going to bite and how," Morgan said locking her eyes with Donovan's.

"Yes, lure with bait. But, we'll be ready. A SWAT team is on the way and will take up their positions in your shed when I give the word. Until then, they will be tourists spending a few hours in a local motel.

"Zach will install microphone chips in the house as soon as we finish this meeting so SWAT can hear from the shed when it starts to go down … starting tomorrow. I figure the bad guys will make their move tomorrow night or the next morning, before mid-day at the latest. Your house was swept earlier when we found the bugs in your phones. Zach and I will be in the house. DelaCruz has to make the first move."

"And how will this lure be put into action?" Stella asked pulling the blanket tight around her, fear returning to her eyes.

"We will give the bad guys a small window of opportunity. So small they will feel they have to act or lose their opportunity. Morgan, in a few minutes you will make two calls on your bugged house phone. I'm sure they will be listening so you have to sound like you mean every word."

"Who do I call?"

"Here's a rough script," Donovan said handing a pad of paper with notes he had been making over the past few hours. "First, you'll call Howard Bond. Read through my notes to get the gist of what I want you to say. Then you will talk to Bond in your own words."

The kitchen was quiet except for a drip, drip, drip, from the leaky faucet that Thaxter had neglected to fix. Morgan finished scanning the notes, looked up at Donovan.

"Then, as you can see on the next page, you'll call your television cable company," Donovan said. "You will report a problem with your cable. Reception is intermittent, acting up. A new renter is coming because you're going away with *Stella*. With what Stella told you and Zach about her situation when you were driving here from the hospital, Bond has an urgent reason to try to eliminate her, this time for good."

Stella let out a gasp, her eyes bulging.

"Sorry, Miss Trent. I'm only trying to impress on both of you the seriousness of what we're asking you to do, asking you to play the part of your lives. In any case, you two are going to be spending a lot of time on the couch watching television."

"The targets!" Morgan said grasping Stella's hand.

Donovan handed the portable wall phone to Morgan. The phone numbers were written at the top of the yellow pad. The script.

"What if it doesn't work?" Zach asked.

"Then we try something else," Donovan replied. "Okay, Morgan. Call Bond."

Morgan pulled herself up straight in the chair and tapped the numbers.

"Hi, Howard. This is Morgan Grant. I'm sure you must be worried sick about Stella ... wondering where she is."

"Ah, yes ... she didn't come home last night. She's never done that before. Did she call you?"

"The police found her ... lying on a snow bank. Howard, I'm very worried about her. The officers took her to the hospital ... she asked for me. I picked her up this morning in Portsmouth. She's with me. She's still very sick ... and afraid of something. I can't get her to talk. I'm going to take her to where it's warm ... Florida."

"Morgan, I can pick her up, take care of her."

"Howard, the police released her into my custody. Once she's feeling better, tells me what happened, I'm sure they will release her in your care. I'm already making arrangements. We're leaving day after tomorrow, late morning. I'll call you when she's settled with me in Florida."

"Morgan, Morgan, where in Florida?"

Disconnecting the call, Morgan sighed in relief. Step one of Donovan's plan was set in motion.

"Okay, Morgan, now call the cable company. You're notifying them of the problem, want it fixed before a new renter comes. Stress that Stella is with you, and that you'll be in and out until tomorrow around five, so anytime from then to the next morning, but before noon, would be the only time."

Morgan made the call. The dispatcher said they would be able to take care of the problem but were booked until ten o'clock the morning she was leaving. And, asked if that was that all right? Morgan agreed to the time, thanked the woman, and hung up.

Zach got up, topped off everyone's coffee, and sat down again.

None of the four spoke. The kitchen was silent except for the drip, drip, drip, of the faucet. All were wondering, but not sharing their thoughts, how Donovan's plan was going to play out.

Donovan stood. He had one more call to make and he wanted it to be in private so he stepped outside. He called Manny Salinas and was not surprised to learn that he, Elizabeth Stitchway, and Macintyre were already in Boston. He told them it might be a good idea if they found a hotel in Portsmouth tomorrow morning. He hoped to call them by tomorrow night or at the very least late the next morning. In answer to Manny's question of where this was going to happen, Donovan replied in York.

Manny had immediately said to heck with Portsmouth, they were heading to York and not to worry, they would not step foot out of the hotel until Donovan called.

The agent swore as he hung up. He had made a mistake. He should not have said anything about York.

———

MENDOZA AND JUNIOR HAD listened, had monitored Morgan's calls. Who was Stella? Was she going to be a problem for Bond? Was he going to renege on their agreement?

Felix drove off the ramp onto I-95 out of Portland. He didn't know the answers to these questions but he was certainly going to find out immediately, before he and Junior arrived in Portsmouth. In less than two hours they would be knocking on Bond's door. Morgan's call to the television company was an unexpected gift. If they needed to take advantage of the gift, they would factor it into their scheme.

Junior by his side, the recording device on the back seat fell silent after Morgan's call to the cable company.

"Doesn't give us much time, Felix. But then York is only twenty minutes from Bond's place as he described it to you."

"I'll call Howard, find out what he says, give you and I time to talk before we see him."

"Good idea. I'd like to hear what he says, particularly about the Stella woman."

Felix picked up his cell from the center console of the car. "Hello, Howard. Felix here. I happened to have some information you might be interested in."

"Okay. What?"

"Who is Stella?"

"My bitch girlfriend. She was … missing. Morgan Grant called me. Stella is with her."

"Ah, you know. Is this a problem for you, Howard, you know … our agreement?"

"No. It's even better. I can take care of both bitches at the same time."

Chapter 51

IF THE LITTLE YELLOW HOUSE on Scituate Road had a heart, it would be pounding against the walls. The house was wired. The house was bugged. People inside were wired. People outside were wired. People down the street were wired. Cars were wired.

Donovan and Zach were positioned in Morgan's bedroom on the second floor with three views of the outside perimeter—left, right, and back.

From the shed, SWAT had the front and back in sight. The team members were wired to hear everyone and everyplace.

Stella and Morgan were at their posts. Jenny was with Harriett. Morgan told her she would pick her up by three the next afternoon at which time Morgan was leaving with Stella en route to Florida to recuperate.

All were read into the story whether they realized it or not.

And so they sat, stood, paced, waited … waited … waited.

SWAT members did not sleep. Zach and Donovan rotated—three hours on duty, three hours off to rest. Energy bars and water were within everyone's reach.

Morgan and Stella tried to rest but the adrenalin kept them alert.

So went the night. Quiet. Uneventful.

The sun rose Wednesday morning shining brightly on the tranquil street, on the little yellow house. A squirrel switched its fluffy tail, chattering to a squirrel on another branch. A rabbit scampered through the underbrush.

At eight o'clock, a black van drove up. A magnetic sign on the two front doors identified the van: York Television Repair. A man in a black jumpsuit, a ball cap pulled low to his eyes, sauntered up to the house carrying a clipboard.

He rang the bell.

"Door's open. Come on in," Morgan called out.

The man entered and in a split second shot two rounds into the back of the heads of a blonde and a brunette sitting on the couch facing the television's snowy screen. As he turned to leave SWAT swarmed through the front and back doors. Startled, the man fired at the first armed man charging at him, his bullet going wide of the mark. In the exchange, the repairman slumped to the floor a quizzical look on his face, staring up at the woman standing over him. "Stella?" he asked in a dying breath.

On the couch, was a blonde wig and brunette wig lying on top of two deflated blowup dolls.

With Zach on his heels, Donovan charged down the stairs yelling. "The street. Check the street. Check the van." SWAT fanned out. Donovan verified that the television repairman was dead.

Zach stood beside Morgan and Stella looking at the body.

Tears erupted from Stella's eyes as she pulled off the ball cap. "It's my Howie."

"Dammit," Donovan said. "Where's the God damn albino?"

Morgan leaned against the doorway. *It's not over.*

Within minutes, the five SWAT members returned to the house. They had done their jobs but they knew in spite of the man on the floor, they didn't get the leader of the cartel, only the man who wanted to be the distributor of weapons from Mexico.

"Agent Donovan, there's a man outside wants to come in. He's in that white Escapade up the road. Says he's a fisherman. Says his name is Mac."

"Mac?" Morgan brushed by the SWAT officer, ran out into the sunshine, up the driveway, up the short distance to the white van. Mac stepped out of the driver's side, catching Morgan in his arms, and into a long embrace before they slid onto the back seat of the car disappearing from everyone's eyes. One SWAT officer stood by the car door. It was nice to see a couple united unharmed.

Zach watched her and turned away.

Donavan watched, smiled, and turned back to the scene in the house. "Okay, guys, bundle the body up for the drop-off at the Boston morgue. On your way, split up. One group going straight to Boston, the other stops in Portsmouth. I want all you can get from Bond's condo. We want the names of the militia members, where the shipment of guns was delivered … anything relating to his operation."

Zach and Donovan stood watching as SWAT pulled on latex gloves and went about their duties: photos of the crime scene including the fizzled blow up dolls, picking up spent bullet cartridges, bagging everything to be cataloged for evidence. Others bundled the body, cleaned the floor, and began transferring the body and the revolver the killer had concealed under the clipboard to their SUV in the garage.

The SWAT leader, cell to his ear, listened to the station commander. A storm had kicked up and was moving west to the coast of Maine. He was told to wrap up the crime scene and head back to base with the body ASAP.

"Agent Donovan, did the couple come in the house … the fisherman and the woman?" the officer yelled, his face stricken by something he saw.

"No. Why?"

"Harry's dead. No one's in the car."

Donovan and Zach raced out, up the street to the white car, to the dead officer lying on the pavement. "Zach, how long were they out here?" Donovan cried out his face red, furious looking at the dead officer.

Zach, his throat constricted, checked his watch not because it was going to tell him anything, but because his mind was jammed with horrible images. Where was his witness, the woman he cared about? He looked up at the gathering gray clouds. A storm was heading their way.

"I don't know. Fifteen minutes … probably longer."

Donovan stood, his cell to his ear giving orders to the dispatcher at the Boston Field office. "Put out an APB for two hostages, a man and woman, a blonde woman. Morgan Grant. You have her picture, complete description on file. The man, wait," Donovan turned to Zach. "Do you have a picture of Macintyre … no?" Donovan turned away, continuing his conversation with the field office. "There's no picture of the man unless Vickers calls to tell you otherwise. I believe the pair was taken by Junior DelaCruz and possibly Felix Mendoza.

"Mendoza's picture is on file. Put up roadblocks immediately, I-95 and Route 1 and 1A, both directions out of York, Maine. Stakeout airports and airstrips, stop and search any train rolling through southern Maine, both directions."

Chapter 52

A POWERBOAT PULLED AWAY from an abandoned dock north of York Harbor. Mendoza was at the wheel of the 1988, twenty-five foot Boston Whaler, with twin outboards. Their two hostages were secured in the small cabin. The plan—speed out three or so miles in the Atlantic and dump the pair.

Tape over their mouths, Mac held Maria's eyes with his, pouring out his love for her as they struggled with the rope that Mendoza had tied around their wrists and ankles. Maria had some strength, but the fingers of a surgeon were not exercised for strength but for accuracy with a scalpel.

Mac's fingers, on the other hand, were strong—battling fish, cleaning fish, constantly wrestling with ropes and the chains of a winch and anchor. His fingers worked the knots. He could feel the rope give, the knot loosening. Cuts in his wrists, blood droplets, didn't stop him. His captor was not a fisherman, not a seaman, so his experience with tying knots was limited.

The boat took the waves head on. They were building. A storm was approaching fast, almost on top of them. Junior yelled at Felix over the noise of the sea to keep pushing on the gas. They had to get rid of their passengers before Donovan and his boys realized they did not escape by car, train, or plane, but had escaped by sea.

The fiberglass hull slammed into the waves making little forward progress. For every yard they advanced they seemed to lose two. Mendoza gripped the wheel trying to keep control of the powerboat. Junior clung to the console rail in front of the navigator's seat beside Felix.

———

DOWN IN THE CABIN Mac broke through the knots on his wrists. He ripped the tape from his mouth. Being as careful as he could, he then removed the tape covering Maria's mouth as she clenched her teeth refusing to make a sound. Mac placed his lips on hers. "I'm sorry if it hurt. I love you."

"I love you, too. Mac—the storm. Can this boat take it?"

"She seems stout … hopefully a bull in this weather, although from the looks in here, she hasn't exactly been maintained by the Admiral of the Navy," Mac said, quickly untying his ankles then attending to Maria's wrists and ankles. "We need lifejackets and weapons," Mac said. "I don't see anything."

"I don't either."

"Wait, the fire extinguisher." Mac released the small tank from the wall.

"Mac, there are storage cabinets overhead."

"You check them. I'll look under the bunks. Yeah, look at this, a tool chest. Screwdriver, not much help. Hammer. A wrench. That's the ticket. Find any lifejackets?"

"Here. Lifejackets," Maria called over her shoulder standing on the edge of a bunk. She pulled two orange jackets from an overhead cabinet, tossing them down to Mac.

"Great. Inflatable. Put this around your neck," he said adjusting the strap and then putting one over his head.

"Mac … I love you. My hair—"

"Silly. Blonde, red, brown, bald, I don't care as long as you're okay. Now we pull the rip cord and pray it works."

They grinned at each other—the orange jackets inflated.

"What do we do now?" Maria asked falling onto the wooden bunk with the lurch of the boat.

"We wait. They're heading into the storm. The waves are getting bigger. This boat is strong, but I doubt they're used to being in a rough sea. We wait. They may get sick. We wait for a wave to knock them over, lose control."

"Can you tell if they lose control, maybe not at the wheel?"

"Yes. I'll take the extinguisher. Here, you take the wrench. Which feels like you have more control? Hammer or wrench? Remember you're going to hit them in the head, kick them in the crotch as if your life depended on it. Can you do that?"

"You bet I can. Oooh—"

"That was a big one. Hold on, I'm going to try the door. Be ready."

Mac saw the albino sliding down the deck on his belly to the stern frantically waving his hands, trying to grab hold of something, anything, terror in his eyes, screaming at Felix to help him. Screaming he feared the water.

"Now, Maria. Now."

Maria didn't hesitate. She followed Mac, wrench in one hand the other splayed on his back to keep her balance.

The fisherman smashed Mendoza on the back of his skull just as his fingers slipped from the wheel. Maria stumbled, dropped the wrench, but managed to grab a gaff secured next to a fishing pole. A wave hit the boat broadside throwing her down to the deck. She looked up just as Junior fell backward against the stern. Struggling to his knees, his pink eyes locked on Maria. He lunged at her.

With a death grip on the gaff, and with all her strength, she slammed the hook end into Junior but it grazed passed his ear. Falling backward, she pulled on it, the stainless steel point sunk into the back of Junior's neck, like a meat hook. Blood spurted as it punctured his carotid artery. His eyes wide in horror, he slumped to the deck, washed against the stern, the gaff impaled through his neck.

Chapter 53

THE MOTORS SPUTTERED, stopped.

Maria looked at Mac.

"What do you want to bet the idiots didn't fill the gas tanks?" Mac yelled. "Hang on I'll take a look." Checking what he could with the boat lurching wildly, there was nothing he could do. The motors did not respond. Mac inched back toward her, grabbed her wrist, pulled her to him, pulled her in front of the captain's chair bolted to the deck of the boat.

Mendoza was lying on the deck, his foot tangled up with the rung of the captain's chair, blood streaming from his head where Mac hit him with the extinguisher. Motioning for her to stay, to hold on to the chair, he retrieved the ropes from the cabin and bound Mendoza's arms to his body, bound his legs together.

Maria, holding the leg of the chair, bent down, felt for his pulse. "He's still alive. Let's get him into the cabin. If he lives, Donovan and Zach can interrogate him. Where's a first aid kit? I need to clean his head, the gash," Maria yelled over the roar of the waves. Pellets of ice mixed with snow pecked at her face.

"Hang on. Probably something in the console ... here. Let's get him below. I'll hand the kit down to you."

"Okay. Mac, I think Junior's dead."

"Yeah, I saw. You did good. I don't know where your strength came from."

"He was coming for me. What do they say about fight or flight? I had to stop him," she shouted.

"I hear you," he yelled back, holding her tighter against him, pressing the two lifejackets flat to each other. "We have to get help. No motor ... we could get swamped. I'm sure they're looking for us, but they don't know where. Might not think to look for us out here. We'll get this guy down below. You look in those cabinets for a flare gun and some flares. They'll be under cover, out of the weather. I'll come back out here, give you the kit, and then check these cabinets for flares. Hopefully, the Coast Guard will find us."

"Let's go. I'm ready," Maria shouted.

Mac lifted Mendoza's shoulders, pulling him down the short stairway gripping his armpits while Maria maneuvered his legs and feet, flopping the large Mexican onto the wooden bunk. Mac hurried back on deck, grabbed the first-aid kit, handing it down to Maria, then set to checking the cabinets in the cockpit for a flare gun.

Like everything else on the boat, Maria saw the kit hadn't been resupplied, but there were alcohol wipes and some antibiotic ointment. It would have to do. The Mexican winced with the sting of the alcohol, but said nothing. Satisfied she had done all she could at the moment, Maria checked his pockets for a cell. Finding one in his pants, she could see it wasn't working, soaked with water. She put it in her pocket and immediately began searching the cabinets for a flare gun.

It was close to six o'clock. The sky and the sea were almost black.

The running lights flickered, the lights on the console flickered, flickered again but stayed on. They had to hurry. With the storm overhead they wouldn't be able to see much longer. The boat's electrical circuits might be damaged, the high waves washing over the deck of the boat, seeping into every nook and cranny.

"Find anything, Maria?" Mac yelled through the door to the cabin below.

"No, wait, is this it? It's a tube thing, three ... no gun. Mac, the lights went out."

"I know. It must be faulty wiring, a bad ground wire. Probably never checked," Mac called back as Maria stepped up to the deck holding three tubes which looked like sticks of dynamite.

"Perfect. Rocket flare with a parachute. Okay, we have three. We don't know how old or if they're going to work. Whoa. That was a big wave. Here, help me stuff them under my jacket. Can't let them get wet. It's almost dark. No planes overhead yet," he yelled wiping water from his face only to be hit by the spray of another monster wave.

"No one's looking for us, Mac." Maria shuddered from the freezing rain and snow whipping against her sweater. Their clothing was woefully lacking. Neither one of them thought they would be out at sea.

"I don't suppose you have your cell on you?" Mac asked with a chuckle.

"Kitchen counter. You?" she yelled.

"Car seat. I checked the ..." he nodded toward the body. "Water knocked it out. Could come back if it dries. Put it in my pocket."

"Me too," she nodded to the stairs. "There are some blankets down below ... saw them near the flares. I'll feel around, get them," Maria said as her body shuddered.

"Why don't you stay there? You'll be out of the wind, and the waves."

"Not on your life, Captain Mac. Not with that Mexican. Like it or not, you're stuck with me."

"Kind of like that," he said gripping her shoulder, placing a quick hot kiss on her lips. "More of that later, doc. Get those blankets. As soon as we see or hear someone looking for us, we'll set off a flare. Here, hang on to my hand."

Gripping Mac's hand until she reached the stairs, she scampered down returning with two blankets.

Bundling themselves in the blankets, Mac sat on the captain's pedestal seat, arms holding Maria against him, both gripping the wheel for support.

"Mac, how did you find me?" Maria shouted.

"Manny and Liz. They talked to Donovan and I'm not sure who else. Good for us, they're in York. They'll find us if the Feds can't."

"Mac, Liz saw me in Boston. I don't know how she knew it was me, but she did. I called her on Christmas day."

"I know. I didn't find out until a few days ago. She confessed."

"What?" Maria shouted over a wave roaring around them.

"I said, she confessed, but that you had sworn her to silence. I was furious inside, but I also understood."

"Mac, she said you and Flo were a couple."

"What?"

"Flo? You?"

"Not when I thought you might be alive," he said in her ear, holding her so tight he thought she might break.

Maria sighed, pressing back against him.

"Hey, do you see a light?" Mac asked.

"Where?"

"Over there, to our right?" Mac said his cheek next to hers, their eyes riveted on the spot, waiting for the next wave to lift the boat. "There."

"Yes. Get the flare." Letting the blanket fall to the deck, Maria reached under his jacket and pulled out one of the flares.

"Okay. Stand clear," Mac said. "We don't know if this thing is going to work." Mac edged to the end of the cockpit. He pulled out the safety pin, extended the firing lever, then pushed the firing lever up against the outer casing. The rocket took off, took off a few yards into the sky, then fell into the water.

Pulling the second flare from under his jacket, he repeated the steps but this time it took off about nine-hundred feet into the sky. Even with the wind and icy rain it could be seen from the boat Mac thought he saw in the distance. That is if they were looking in the right direction. The rocket slowly descended to the water, sometimes carried up by the wind, then dropping again.

"Do you think they saw it, Mac?" Maria shouted, holding onto the wheel with all her strength trying not to look at the body in the stern. Another gust of wind and large waves slammed against the boat.

"I don't know. We'll wait a few minutes. If we see the light again, we'll set off our last one."

Once again bundling themselves with the blankets, Mac on the captain's pedestal seat, arms wrapped tight around Maria, they kept their eyes peeled for the elusive light.

"There. There it is. Shoot off another flare, Mac."

"It's our last."

"I know. Do it."

Again letting his blanket drop to the deck, he fired off their last rocket. It went higher than the others, seemed to hang in the wind longer. Maria didn't watch the rocket. Her eyes were riveted on the angry sea. "Please, dear God, let them find us," she whispered.

"Maria, the boat. The lights flashed. They saw us. I'm sure of it," he yelled bundling her up again, arms holding her tight, saying a silent prayer that he wasn't hallucinating.

Slowly the light came closer. "It's the Coast Guard. Maria, they found us."

Chapter 54

IT SEEMED TO TAKE forever for their rescuers to close the distance to the floundering Whaler. Finally the Coast Guard cutter pulled as close as they dared, hampered by the stormy sea. Transferring the pair onto the cutter was not going to be an easy task. Maria was first, strapped into a harness. Bumping her legs, then arms, she was finally pulled onto the deck of the ship falling into a seaman's arms. He immediately bundled her into a blanket.

"Were you on patrol when you saw the flare?" she shouted.

"No. We were looking for you. Some private investigator, a woman, called telling us there were hostages out in this storm."

Maria, clutching the blanket, looked at him in disbelief as another seaman swung precariously toward the Boston Whaler. Mac grabbed his legs hanging from the harness pulling him onto the deck. Maria saw Mac point to the dead man, the gaff still in place, and then pointed to the cabin below where there was a man clinging to life. She and Mac had discussed it was vital the boat be towed to shore. It was a crime scene and as such held critical evidence, evidence, the Feds would desperately need.

The seaman radioed back to the skipper on the cutter to prepare to tow the crippled Whaler back to the station.

———

PULLING INTO THE BRIGHT floodlights of the Coast Guard Station, Maria spotted Zach and Agent Donovan in a heated discussion, then Manny and Liz. Liz was waving, jumping up and down, yelling something when she saw Maria on the deck of the cutter.

Taking the hand of a seaman, Maria stepped onto the dock, falling into Liz's embrace. Then it was Zach's turn, grasping her tight, tears streaming down her face.

"Are you all right?" he asked wiping the tears from her cheeks. "Did they hurt you?"

"I'm okay, but it was scary, horrible—the storm, DelaCruz, the other guy."

"Morgan, are you okay?" Agent Donovan said pulling her arm away from Zach.

Everyone was talking slowly, yelling, over the engine of the cutter, the howling wind, faces frozen from the icy air. The blanket draped around Maria flapped with each gust. The engine stopped, but the howl of the wind continued.

"Alex, DelaCruz is dead. I killed him," Maria mouthed through a fresh rush of tears. "Where's Mac?"

"Right here, Maria. Right here." He pulled her away from Donovan and into his arms. Holding her blanketed head to his chest, they clung to each other. "I love you. Thank God you're safe. It's over, Maria."

"I know. I love you, Mac."

Easing her back, Mac smeared the stream of tears away from eyes. "I have to go back to Boston tonight. Donovan called me while we were being towed. I have to give a statement as to what happened, how they took us, and … what happened on the boat."

"Mac, I've killed two men," she whispered in his ear, her body trembling.

"You did what you had to do, Maria. You've been trained to act, no matter the circumstances, And, thank God you did."

"But, Mac—"

He held her close. "It's okay. It's okay."

Seeing the red and blue lights flashing through the icy rain, they glanced over to the Whaler. The big guy Mac hit on the head, laying on a stretcher, was being loaded into an EMT van.

Mac kissed the top of her head, caressed her blonde hair. "Manny and Liz are registering at a hotel … and getting me a room. We're flying to Tampa after I've answered all of Donovan's questions. I wanted to stay with you but Donovan said it was imperative I talk with him immediately, and to let you wrap up here. He suggested I should wait for you in Florida. What do you want me to do?" Mac asked.

Maria stepped away, looked at the snow swirling on the ground. "Florida is best. I was thinking on the Coast Guard boat, realizing we were safe, that my nightmare was over, I let myself think about what was next. Mac, I will be leaving a piece of my life here—people. There are goodbyes. Wait for me in Cortez, on your boat, the Patty Sue. Less than two weeks."

"I'll hold you to that or I'm racing back to get you. I love you Dr. Maria Grayson."

"And, I love you, Captain Mac."

Epilogue

THE LITTLE YELLOW HOUSE was cloaked in sleepy silence. The storm had blown out to sea.

U.S. Marshal Zachary Vickers, sitting at the kitchen table in his sock feet, was talking on his cell to Agent Alex Donovan in hushed tones, pausing for an occasional sip of piping hot coffee. Donovan was relating a list of tasks the two officers had to perform: processing the bodies—Thaxter, Bond, and the body he was sure was DelaCruz; interrogating Felix Mendoza now in custody at York Hospital waiting for an ambulance to transport him to a hospital near the Boston Field Office. Vickers was to arrange a meeting at the field office. The task: processing Morgan Grant out of the Witness Protection Program.

It was after midnight. Morgan and Stella were lying in Morgan's queen-sized bed staring at the ceiling, whispering back and forth like school girls on a sleepover but without the giggling. They were sharing thoughts on the events that had taken place the past twenty-four hours. Morgan reunited with her lover, Stella losing her lover. Howard Bond shot dead now lying in a Boston morgue guarded by a federal agent until all evidence and forensics were taken.

"Stella, what are you going to do?" Morgan asked.

"Move back to York, stay with my parents until I find a place. Ask my boss at the office supply store if I can have my old job back. He may have found a replacement. I guess you'll be leaving?"

"Yeah." Morgan rolled over propping her head on her hand. Stella did the same, the two friends facing each other. Morgan had turned the electric blanket on high. She wasn't sure if she would ever be warm again. Stella's feet protruded from underneath the covers to cool off.

"It happened so fast. Today. Not all the months before," Morgan said softly touching Stella's hand.

"What about your friends, the private investigators? They seemed nice," Stella whispered.

"Stel, they're wonderful. Donovan arranged for an agent to escort Mac to the Boston Field Office to take his statement. Which, I guess, will take most of the night and morning. Liz and Manny are going with him, stay the night in Boston, and then the three of them will return to Florida."

"I bet your man, who, by the way, is out of this world sexy. Anyway, I bet he didn't want to leave you."

"And vice-versa. It was hard to say goodbye again, but it won't be too long." Morgan sighed, rolling on her back. "I explained that I had to wrap up this life, say goodbye to people I counted as friends. A few days maybe. Then I'll be racing back to Cortez … to Mac."

Stella didn't answer. She was asleep, breathing easy.

Morgan slipped out of bed, put on her robe and quietly went down the stairs to the kitchen. The door was open a crack allowing a slice of light to fall across the hardwood floor.

"Can I join you?" she asked smiling at Zach, pen raised in the air as she helped herself to coffee. Zach was in his sock feet, heel tapping the floor.

The atmosphere was warm, chummy. They had been through a lot together, now relaxed in each other's company.

"How are you feeling, Morgan," Zach asked.

"Wonderful … I think. Yes, wonderful. Tomorrow I start saying goodbye to Morgan Grant's friends—Dr. Farnsworth, Harriett … a couple others."

"Alex and I were discussing over the phone how to process you out of the program," Zach said. "Unless, of course, you decide to stay in Maine."

Morgan rolled her eyes. "Not in this lifetime. But, thanks for the offer. How long will it take—the mustering out procedure?"

"A few hours. We need your statement … add what took place over the last few weeks from your perspective, to the video we took before. Sign some papers. Are you going to fly to Florida? What about Jenny?" he asked.

"I think I'll rent a car. Easier to drive with her. I didn't buy any furniture, oh the loveseat upstairs, but that's it … some clothes. A few days, maybe a week, to put Morgan's life in order, then drive to

Boston to meet with you and Donovan. How does that sound? I'll know better by this afternoon...after I talk to Richard."

"He may ask you to stay a couple of weeks," Zach said topping off his coffee.

"I'll see. I don't want to leave him shorthanded, but he has to understand that I'm not hanging around here. I like Maine ... another life maybe, but it's not home."

"I'm going out as soon as the Bagel Basket opens, pick up the works for breakfast," Zach said. "You and Stella will be hungry once the sun rises. Then I'll be heading back to Boston. Are you okay here alone, after ... you know ... what happened in the house?"

"Stella will be staying with me until I leave York. I suppose you're going to have to take her statement, too. Howard kept her in the dark, but she's smart. She may know more about his contacts than she thinks she does."

On his way to the Bagel Basket, Zach picked up Jenny. Harriett wanted to chat, asking questions about the story playing over and over on the television morning news. Was it true about Morgan? Zach just smiled, clipped the leash on Jenny's collar, telling Harriett she'd have to wait for Morgan.

Goodbye!

By eleven o'clock Morgan was ready to say goodbye to Richard and Harriett. With Jenny on her leash, she entered the practice. Richard was waiting for her as was Harriett, both sitting in his office, faces crestfallen.

Jenny rushed to Harriett, slapped her muzzle down on her lap asking for her treat. Harriett petted her and cooed, that, yes, she had a biscuit for the pretty girl.

Richard spoke first. Morgan sat opposite Harriett both looking at him across his desk.

"Well, I guess I knew you were too good to be true."

The morning news reported over and over what happened the day and night before. Nothing about the murders, only revealing the double life of Morgan Grant living in their midst. A real hero, the reporters related, in the U.S. Government's Witness Protection Program.

"The reports are that your home is in Florida, near Tampa, a little fishing village, Cortez," Richard said. "I guess that means you'll be leaving us."

"Yes. Richard, you've been wonderful, Harriett, you too. Please don't think I'm ungrateful, but I am anxious to return to my home. Can you understand that?"

"Yes, my dear, and I think I speak for Harriett, we understand. Don't worry about us. The hospital is sending over a nurse until I can find a permanent replacement for you. I know that will be impossible. I suppose this is goodbye, but we want to hear from you. Please don't be a stranger."

"Morgan, I knew there was something different about you. You were so competent, carried yourself with such strength, but I would never have come up with a double life. The paper said your real name is Maria Grayson, Dr. Maria Grayson?"

"That's right, but while the Witness Protection provided all the papers, found this job for me, I did pass the Maine Boards. So, I guess Dr. Morgan Grant exists. I'll have to sort that out, merging my identities into one. I'll let you know how that shakes out and—"

The door flew back on its hinges. Barly barged into the office, took Morgan by the arm, stood her up and propelled her into the nearest examination room. "Excuse us, but I'd like to talk to Morgan privately," he said over his shoulder.

"So, you're a government witness, your name is Maria Grayson, Dr. Grayson, a surgeon?" Barly stood, feet apart, arms across his chest facing her—both in the middle of the small room, like prize fighters ready to spar in the ring.

"That about covers it, Barly," Morgan answered softly, stepping back, leaning against the wall.

Barly hiked himself up on the end of the examination table, the paper crinkling under his weight, the stirrups for a woman's examination turned down to the floor.

"When are you leaving?" he asked the words catching in his throat.

"Tomorrow, maybe the next day, depends on how quickly I can wrap things up here, a car …"

Barly sat, his fingers gripping the edge of the table, staring at her. He wasn't glaring, wasn't mad, he was beaten. "If you ever want to come back, I'll be here. If you ever need help, call me. I won't call you. You have a life and from what I heard on the news, you also have a fisherman by the name of Macintyre. I won't intrude. I was part of Morgan Grant's life. Not the other one. Promise you'll call if you need my help?"

Morgan nodded. Tears pooling in her eyes as the memories of their friendship and brief encounter rushed in. Suddenly everything was very difficult.

Barly slid off the exam table, wrapped her gently in his arms, tucking her blonde curls under his chin. Breathing slowly, he released her, kissed her forehead, and left.

———

SALLY SLATHERED ON THE hair color returning Morgan Grant to the auburn Maria Grayson. For the first time ever, Sally permitted a dog in her shop. Morgan promised Jenny would lie down on her blanket in the corner while Sally worked her magic.

Finished with the slathering, the waiting, the clipping, Sally twirled Morgan around so she could see all sides of her new do. "What do you think, hon? You double agent girl. Honestly, Morgan, I couldn't believe what that reporter was saying on the morning news. My jaw dropped. And to think you were right here in my chair when you changed your look. I know now you didn't want those bad men to find you. Honestly, I told my husband, if they had barged into my shop shooting, I would have fallen to the floor bullet or no bullet."

"You've been wonderful, Sally, and I think the color is very close to what I was. Besides the federal agents, you were the only one in York who saw me before I turned into a blonde."

"Tell me, hon. Do blondes have more fun?"

"Sally, it certainly added to the mix."

Morgan settled up with Sally including a large tip. She called Jenny, picked up her blanket, and gave Sally a final hug before scooting out the door. Looking out the car's back window at Sally, standing in the snow waving goodbye, the little shop began to recede, then disappeared. Morgan drove to I-95 leaving the village of York in her rearview mirror.

Released from the
Witness Protection Program!

A few more hours and Morgan Grant would cease to exist. It was a wonderful feeling. Parking in the Boston garage for the last time, her step was quick as she walked to Zach's Field Office, Jenny trotting beside her on the leash. Taking the elevator to the secure office area, she was greeted with a hug from Zach as well as Agent Donovan. Her auburn hair and violet eyes were not lost on the two officials.

They guided her into the conference room where several sheets of paper requiring her signature were laid out on the table.

"This won't take long, Morgan," Donovan said giving Jenny a pat. "By the way you may be interested to know that the print from the Cortez double murder—"

"Studs?" she asked.

"Yes, Studs and Wallace Gutfeld. The third print matched the set of prints we were able to get from DelaCruz's hand."

"You don't have to explain, Alex. I was there. I ... I saw him."

"Yes, of course. Anyway we now have proof that he murdered the two men. We also have your testimony so that case is closed— the Perez murder and the other two in Cortez. We have had a bit of luck with the Mexican, Felix Mendoza. He cut a deal with us. If we protect him, he'll give us everything about the DelaCruz cartel's gun running business as well as marijuana. Drug trafficking. He definitely identified the albino as Junior DelaCruz."

"That is great news. Have you talked to Stella?" Morgan asked smiling at the two men.

"Yes, on the phone. She's coming in tomorrow so we can videotape her statement," Zach said.

"Want to take a last look at the case board?" Donovan asked as he brought up the file on the electronic white board.

Morgan nodded, pouring a cup of coffee from the carafe on a side table. Nodding to the two men, she added hot coffee to their now tepid cups. Zach absently scratched Jenny's ears as he took a sip from his mug.

Case: DelaCruz Cartel

<u>Target:</u> Junior DelaCruz, dead	<u>Believed he killed:</u>	<u>Known Bugs</u>
<u>Crime:</u> Murder, Gun Running, Drugs	√Perez	Mother-2
<u>Last seen:</u> Anna Maria Island, FL, 7 months ago	√Studs	Mac-2
	√Wally	Morgan-3

<u>Persons of Interest</u>

Felix Mendoza: in custody, protected witness

Howard Bond: dead

Paul Thaxter: dead

Junior DelaCruz: dead

Case closed: murder of Arturo Perez

Morgan Grant returns to Dr. Maria Grayson

—   —   ...

Donovan updated the names, their status, and that the case of the Arturo Perez murder was closed. "I spoke with Thaxter's boss. He said that Paul had fed them bits of information, enough so they thought maybe he was okay but not enough to allay their suspicions. Thaxter had given the ATF Mendoza's picture and his full name. Also, the ATF had been gathering information on Bond. Evidently Bond didn't know the identity of the so-called rancher. So, with the possession of Bond's computer from his condo, they found his activities with various militia groups including Bond's purchase of weapons through Thaxter, and the subsequent sale to his clients. Stella's statement will be helpful—she overheard some of Bond's conversations."

Then it was Morgan's turn to speak. Zach turned on the video camera, and he and Donovan listened to Morgan's statement interspersing with a few questions for clarification, recording everything for the record.

She told them she and Mac were vaguely aware that a car or van had driven up. "Somebody lost, asking directions. We didn't pay any attention. There was an officer close by. Two men, I guess they took out the officer. We weren't aware, didn't hear anything. They overpowered us ... one of them opened the car door and stabbed a needle in Mac's back, the other one stabbed a needle in my shoulder as he leaned over the front seat. The next thing we knew we were in the cabin of a boat. Our wrists and ankles were tied and tape covered our mouths."

She sighed. Did she really have to tell about how she killed the man with pink eyes lunging at her?

Donovan looked up. "Briefly, just briefly tell us about the two men ... enough to corroborate what Macintyre told us."

She did what Donovan asked. Briefly.

The room fell silent. The picture she painted was vivid. There were no questions.

Finished, Donovan turned off the video-cam as Zach moved the papers in front of Morgan, handing her a pen. He watched her sign her release from the program, and her exit from his life. His heels weren't bouncing on the floor. He had no energy to move any part of his body. He wished with all his heart he had met Morgan at a different time and under different circumstances.

With a hug for Zach, a handshake with Donovan, Dr. Maria Grayson, Jenny by her side, left the Boston Field Office and their lives.

I'm back!

Mac was sitting up on the flying bridge of the Patty Sue, the captain's seat, turned to face the dock leading to the parking lot, leading to Maria.

Manny and Liz were part of the welcoming party. They sat in the stern, their chairs maneuvered so they too could look up the dock. Danny stood behind them leaning against the door frame leading down to the galley. He fiddled with the line on a fishing pole not daring to look. Maybe Maria wouldn't show, like his Patty Sue didn't show so many years ago. He prayed that wouldn't be the case for his son.

Mac was the first to see her. She was running down the weathered dock, her high-heels swinging from her fingers, a large tote swinging under her arm, the white blouse, the sleeves and the fabric of her slacks, catching the air as she ran. Jenny's soft golden ears were flopping as she galloped beside her mistress.

Mac was off the boat in a flash, running up to meet her, catching her in his arms, swinging her around, both laughing. He set her on her feet, holding her tight, never ever to let go again. They kissed. They hugged. They laughed.

Mac pointed to the Patty Sue, to the welcoming party standing mesmerized by the couple's reunion. Tears streamed down Danny's face, Manny's arm around Liz.

Dr. Maria Grayson was back!

Mac helped her onto the Patty Sue as Jenny made a flying leap to the deck. Everyone lined up with more hugs, more kisses, Jenny darting from one human to the next receiving pats and ear scratches.

Sunbeams streamed down from the cloudless blue sky, sending crystal rainbows off each ripple into the air.

It was a great day for a homecoming. Manny and Elizabeth Salinas stood silently, Liz holding Danny's hand, his tears still flowing.

Taking Maria's hand, Mac led her up to the flying bridge, waved at his pops and Manny to untie the ropes as he started the engine. The Patty Sue responded, churning the water as she slowly pulled away from the dock. Mac held Maria in front of him as he had done on the hostage boat, but this time, this day, she was his.

——

AN HOUR OUT AT SEA, Danny called up to Mac. "Ready for the champagne?"

"Drop the anchor, we'll be right down."

Mac cut the engines, letting the Patty Sue roll leisurely on the waves against the tug of the anchor.

"Mac, before we join the others, I have something to show you." Maria reached into her large bag pulling out sheets of folded yellow paper tied together with a white ribbon. She handed the packet of letters to Mac, nodding that he should untie the ribbon. The letters were for him as was the envelope with a slight bulge on top.

He opened the envelope and the small conch shell he had given her on the sandbar almost a year ago, the sandbar where he made love to her, fell into his hand. He looked up fingering the smooth pearly surface—she was looking back at him, both remembering the moment.

Mac took her hand and put the shell in her palm closing her fingers.

A wave of warmth flowed through her, but she had more to share. "I began writing a sort of journal. But I felt so bad being torn from my home, torn from you, that it made me feel better if I wrote to you about what was happening to me. You'll see that as time went on, I changed the words I used to sign off. My feelings for you were real, deeper, knowing, realizing how much I love you."

"What's this? Christmas you switch to Dear Diary?"

"That was a dreadful day, the day I called Liz and Manny to wish them a merry Christmas. Actually that was a ruse. I really wanted to know how you were. Liz told me about Flo. It sounded as if you were going to marry her."

Mac gazed into her eyes. "I never really believed you were … gone. But as time went on I began to think maybe you were … that I should move on."

"But you didn't. What stopped you?"

Mac looked to the few fluffy clouds scuttling in the sunlight. "Remember that psychic … Crystal?" he chuckled.

"Yes, but—"

"Honest to God, Maria, it was crazy, like it was meant to happen. I was having dinner with Flo at the Sandbar. Crystal makes a beeline for me, bumps my arm and whispers in my ear that you're alive and then she disappears. I wanted to believe her but I didn't know what to do, how to find you. I called Manny and Liz. Luckily, I guess things were beginning to happen in the case, most of which I didn't know about until lately.

"Maria, you came back, you came back for a reason. We were meant to be together. Please stay with me, live with me." Mac wrapped her in his arms, his heart beating against hers. "Maria, marry me."

Maria nodded. "Yes … yes, I'll marry you."

"Hey up there, are we going to drink this champagne by ourselves," Danny called up laughing with Liz and Manny.

"I guess maybe we should join the party," Maria said.

"Dr. Grayson, after a couple glasses of champagne, don't you forget you said yes to my proposal."

"Not a chance of that happening."

Mac took her hand as they climbed down from the flying bridge, she still in her bare feet.

"About time you two joined us," Danny said.

Maria and Mac accepted the glasses of champagne from Manny tapping each other's glass in a silent toast.

"Mac, I can't tell you how happy I was to see you that morning, that is, before we were kidnapped. But how did you know where I—"

"We traced your call," Manny said. "When you called to wish Stitch and I a merry Christmas, I saved it. Then when Donovan let it slip that things were happening in York, I pulled up your call, the address."

"I couldn't wait," Mac said holding his glass out to Manny for a refill. I was only going to drive to your street, never get near the house, but ... well, that's when one of the officers saw the car. We all know what happened after that."

Maria, holding her glass to Manny to top off her glass with the golden bubbly, turned to Liz. "Liz, a seaman on the Coast Guard boat told me a private investigator, a woman, told them to look for the hostages out in the water. You're the only woman investigator I know. If it was you, how did you know to look for me and Mac on the water?" Maria asked petting Jenny leaning against her legs.

"Easy peasy. No one was having any luck finding you guys, so I called our psychic friend. Crystal said she would call me back ... had to meditate."

Manny chimed in. "When she called us back she was almost hysterical, crying. She said Mac was in grave danger. Water around him and a woman. *They* are in grave danger. So, yes, it was Stitch who alerted the Coast Guard. We were just thankful they took her tip seriously."

"Crystal sure had that right," Liz said lifting her glass. "Here's to Crystal."

"To Crystal," Mac said, kissing Maria. "Well, Pops, everybody, I have news for you. I asked Maria to marry me, and she said yes. How about that?"

Tears again flowed down Danny's face as he hugged Maria, kissed both of her cheeks. Then he hugged his son as Liz and Manny took turns hugging Maria and congratulating Mac.

"Well, I guess this calls for another bottle of champagne, wouldn't you say, Mrs. Salinas?" Manny said reaching into the cooler.

"You got that right, Mr. Salinas. Pop that cork."

Manny's arm around Liz, Liz's arm around Danny, they raised their glasses, "To Mac and Maria."

Golden bubbles swirling in her glass, Maria's violet eyes filled with love for her fisherman. Mac tapped her glass, "I love you. Welcome back."

The End

REVIEW REQUEST

If you enjoyed this book, please consider leaving an honest review on Amazon, even if it is only a line or two. It would mean a lot to me—what did you like best about the book, the characters? I would appreciate it very much. Reader reviews are the lifeblood of an author's career. For a long-ago typewriter-jockey like myself, getting a review means a lot.

It's easy. Log into Amazon, search for the book. **TAP** Customer Reviews at the top of the page. **Click**: Write a Customer Review.

Thank you!

ADD ME TO YOUR MAILING LIST

Please shoot me an email to be added to the list for future book launches:

MaryJane@MaryJaneForbes.com

Website: MaryJaneForbes.com

ACKNOWLEDGEMENTS

Again my reviewers came to my aid, saving me from embarrassing mistakes.

Peggy Keeney: Thanks for your tenacious editing. Our discussions, over a mug of coffee, or a glass of wine, made for a far better read and a good time while considering your findings.

Sue Currier: Thanks for apprising me of the intricacies of seaplane charters up and around Moosehead Lake. Currier's Flying Services, Inc, Greenville Junction, ME.

Geri and Dick Rogers: Thanks for your review spotting several errors and faulty assumptions on my part.

Roger and Pat Grady: Thank you for reviewing the manuscript, tracking down inconsistencies and sections requiring more explanation.

Molly Tredwell: Thank you for your help in moving the characters along on their emotional journey. I could never do this without your support.

Next Book: <u>Twists of Fate</u>
TWIST OF FATE SERIES, BOOK 3

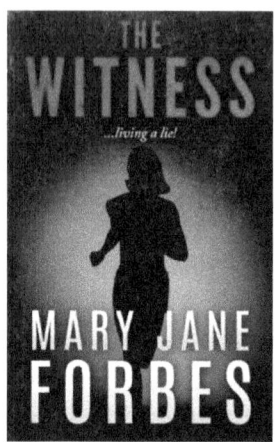

The woman he thought he knew. The man she couldn't leave. A future neither of them could ever have imagined.

After Dr. Maria Grayson took down the Mexican drug lord who wanted her dead, she thought she'd live the rest of her days in peace alongside the fisherman who stole her heart. But when tragedy strikes again, she returns to the small town that gave her shelter in her darkest hour. Unburdened of her old alias, Maria hopes to find acceptance for her true self... especially from the hunky surgeon who fills her fantasies.

Even after all her lies, Dr. Joe "Barly" Bartholomew can't get his mind off the mysterious woman with two names. And he can't help admire the grand entrance she makes when she rushes into a burning church to save multiple children. When the now-fatherless siblings end up in his hospital's burn ward, his frequent visits with the kids only make him fall deeper in love with the woman who saved their lives.

But when a crooked agency threatens the children they've grown to love, Maria and Barly must work together to solve a terrifying mystery and secure their second chance at a new beginning.

Twists of Fate...Dare to Dream is the third book in the fiery Twists of Fate romantic suspense trilogy. If you like gripping medical drama, second chance love stories, and fast-paced action, then you'll love Mary Jane Forbes' captivating mystery.

Buy *Twists of Fate…Dare to Dream* to light the spark on a spectacular romantic suspense story today!

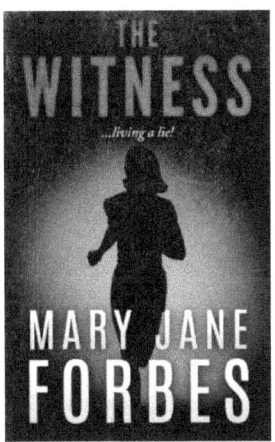

Books by Mary Jane Forbes

Bradley Farm Series
Bradley Farm, Sadie, Finn
Jeli, Marshall, Georgie

The Baker Girl
One Summer, Promises

Twists of Fate Series
The Fisherman, a love story
The Witness, living a lie
Twists of Fate, daring to dream

Murder by Design, Series:
Murder by Design
Labeled in Seattle
Choices, And the Courage to Risk

Elizabeth Stitchway, PI, Series
The Mailbox, Black Magic,
The Painter, Twister

House of Beads Mystery Series
Murder in the House of Beads
Intercept, Checkmate
Identity Theft

Novels - standalone
The Baby Quilt ... a mystery!
The Message...Call Me!

Short Stories
Once Upon a Christmas Eve, a Romantic Fairy Tale
The Christmas Angel and the Magic Holiday Tree

Visit: www.MaryJaneForbes.com

www.ingramcontent.com/pod-product-compliance
Lightning Source LLC
Chambersburg PA
CBHW060257150626
46556CB00021B/556